KATO

Cover design and typesetting by Geoffrey Bunting
Cover image by Trevor Bowman

ISBN 978-1-967756-02-5

First Edition

Published by Otis West
OtisWestBooks.com

Author's Note

I wrote this novel shortly after moving to Seattle in 2000. For years it existed only on a floppy disk, half-forgotten in the back of my desk drawer. It is presented here in its original form—a time capsule from a bygone era.

KATO

A NOVEL

OTIS WEST

One

I pulled up in front of Dan's house and shut off the engine, catching the wipers mid-sweep. And then all I could hear was the soft tapping of rain on the hood and sunroof and, from down the street, the sound of wind chimes.

Ballard was only a few minutes from downtown Seattle, but it was a whole different world. Small two-story houses on narrow lots, separated by chain-link fences. A giant Longs Drugs sign towered over the neighborhood. Turn the corner and you had a gas station and a donut shop and a deli that sold lutefisk.

Still, the neighborhood was changing. Dan's house was one of the only rentals on a block that was slowly becoming more upscale. Several of the houses had been extensively remodeled and many had fresh paint and new cars parked out front. Dan's house, on the other hand, looked like it was about to slump over. The porch was crooked, the paint was peeling, and the roof was covered with a large blue tarp.

So here I was.

Everything had happened very quickly. When I came home from work on Friday, Sara announced that she wanted to have "a talk." Well, we had the talk, and the next day I called Dan, who immediately offered me a room in his basement. So now it was Sunday, and I was actually moving in. It was real.

So far, though, I didn't feel too upset. I was just kind of stunned. There was almost something funny about it all—I mean, if you could stand back and look at it. But I wasn't ready to stand back just yet. I was still doing the stunned thing. I was like someone who had lost their arm—just kind of staring at the stump in a confused sort of way, wondering when it would start to hurt.

Dan had warned me that the only person who would be home was Darryl, and I had already noted the presence of his battered van parked across the street. The guy was a baker, so his hours were all fucked up—he slept during the day and worked at night. I needed to be quiet, because rule number one of staying here was: don't piss off Darryl.

Luckily, I didn't have much stuff. I shuttled everything onto the porch and then, as quietly as I could, I opened the front door and pushed it all inside.

The house was dark and quiet. The living room was like a jungle. Dan's mom was a realtor, and her clients were always leaving her with their abandoned plants. She usually kept the best ones for herself and then gave the rest to Dan. This had been a death sentence until recently, when Ken the freaky landscape architecture student moved in. Ken applied everything he had learned in his horticulture classes to the sickly, root-bound plants. He started pruning them and repotting them and feeding them all sorts of nutrients. Now it was difficult to walk through the room without brushing a large leaf or being snagged by a sticky tendril.

Darryl's room was directly across from the living room. Ken's room was down the hall and Dan slept upstairs under a low, slanted roof. I was going to be sharing a windowless basement room with a band called Ramcharger (they were named after the drummer's truck). Actually, I wasn't sharing the room with the band—according to Dan, they rarely practiced. I was sharing it with their equipment.

I stepped as quietly as I could across the creaky wood floors and managed to get all my stuff downstairs in three trips. Here's what I had: a sleeping bag, three garbage bags filled with clothes, a box of tapes and CDs, two boxes of books and a banker's box filled with files and junk mail and miscellaneous crap. At first I had tried to sort through some of my stuff, but then I was like, fuck it—just box it up. Of course, there was a lot of stuff that was "ours" that I had left behind—the bed, the couch, the stereo and TV. Whatever. I like to think that I'm a Zen kind of guy. You can't weigh me down with a load of crap.

So, not too much stuff, but the question was: where to put it? The room was literally crammed wall to wall with band equipment. I'd only heard Ramcharger once (playing in a pizza parlor over in the University District) and they sucked. At that time they were doing the typical Seattle grunge thing, but Dan told me they'd recently switched to rockabilly. You wouldn't know it from looking at all their stuff—it was still basically standard-issue wanna-be rockstar crap. There were two giant Marshall stacks, numerous sticker-covered guitars and basses, a few duct-taped mic stands, a PA and a battered-looking four-track. The floor was covered with cables and cords and various distortion pedals—I practically twisted my ankle on a bright green Ibanez Tube Screamer. And then there was the drum kit.

I'd played drums just long enough in high school to know that that this was one fucking kickass set. It was an old Slingerland kit, with two sixteen-inch floor toms, Buddy Rich style. I sat down and grabbed the sticks. I was about to let fly when I remembered that Darryl was asleep in the room above me. And even though the walls had been soundproofed with yellowed foam cushions and giant purple egg cartons, I didn't feel like testing it out.

I'd never met Darryl. I'd seen him once in the kitchen drinking a glass of milk, but we had never been formally introduced. Or maybe we had but I had been too stoned to remember.

Still, I knew enough to know I didn't like him. He was a weird, hermit-like fucker with the creepy demeanor of a child molester. He'd been living in this house a long time—something like ten years. In fact, Dan and Ken paid their rent to Darryl, and Darryl dealt with the landlord. Dan suspected that he and Ken were basically splitting the rent for the house—that Darryl was living in the house for free. But Dan didn't care because it was still cheap as hell. Dan and I hadn't discussed what I would be paying, if anything. The plan was for me to crash here for a while and see how it went.

I went back upstairs and sat on the living room couch. The couch was big and yellow and smelled like mildew and disinfectant. There was a large, oblong stain from when someone had puked on it at a party—a yellow stain on a yellow couch. I remembered that party—remembered the guy who had barfed. Now that I thought about it, it must have been before Sara and I started going out. Though Sara had agreed to come to a few parties at Dan's house, she always made us leave before the barfing started.

I sank back into the couch and closed my eyes. Sara and I had been together for two years. Two twenty-fifths of my whole life. What is that? Eight percent? Depending on how you look at it, it either seemed like a lot or it seemed like nothing at all.

Two years. Two years since I had shared a house with a bunch of guys. Two years since I'd lived with the smell of stale beer and cigarettes, sinks filled with dishes, empty refrigerators and dirty bathrooms. Two years since I'd dealt with people crashing around at odd hours, TV and music wars, and arguments over phone bills. I knew I didn't want to stay here long, but right now it was my only option.

I heard a drawer open and close in Darryl's room. Then a cough. I didn't really feel like dealing with the guy yet—I wasn't even sure if Dan had told him that I was moving in. I had been hoping that Dan would show up so he could tail me back to the apartment to return Sara's car. But fuck it. I still had to get my brother's BMX bike—I hadn't been able to fit it into the car with the rest of my stuff. I could just ride the bike back to the house.

I pushed the Civic hard through traffic, swinging around SUVs and accelerating past buses. Sara had bought this car the year before to drive to her job in Redmond. I didn't have a car—hadn't had one since some idiot slammed into my cool old Dart when it was parked on the street and totaled it. I didn't really need a car, though—I took the bus to work.

I didn't understand the whole new car thing—the Armor All on the dashboard, the Scotchgard-treated seats. Sara insured it to the max and worried about every little nick or scratch. The bumper sticker was the worst: Practice Random Acts of Kindness and Senseless Acts of Beauty. It was the kind of "don't worry, be happy" politically correct bullshit that people put on their cars after being hippies in college, before they started working for Microsoft.

I turned on the radio, which Sara kept tuned to NPR. I'd always made fun of the stuck up, nasally dorks on All Things Considered, but now it seemed oddly poetic, part of my little farewell to the Honda, NPR, and Practice Senseless Acts of whatever.

At a stop light I shifted it into park and started revving the hell out of the engine. Did this thing have a rev limiter? I got it up to about 6000 rpm and then the needle bounced back. You can't hurt these new cars.

Someone behind me honked. The light was green.

Seattle. I still felt like a California boy. My stepdad Phil was an engineer—he did completely un-politically correct defense contractor stuff. He got transferred up to the Pacific Northwest from San Luis Obispo when I was in middle school. We moved to Tacoma, a pathetic excuse for a town about an hour south of Seattle. My little brother

Nick (my half-brother) was eight or nine at the time, so he didn't care. But I was bummed. I was bummed that I was away from my old friends and away from my dad (after we left, he moved to Colorado to pursue his life-long dream of becoming a white-water kayak instructor). I was so bummed that all I did in high school was smoke pot. That's how Dan and I got to be friends. His family had also just moved to Tacoma—from Minnesota. And so we hung out together and smoked a lot of pot.

We both ended up going to college together at UW, but soon we drifted apart, and then Dan dropped out at the end of the first year. But after college—after I finished my useless degree in English literature—we started hanging out again.

In a way, Dan was responsible for my breakup with Sara. Sara hated him. She said that I changed when I was around him—she said that when we were together, I turned into a shallow asshole. But I think it was the other way around: I think I changed when I was with her.

The truth was, Sara and I were very different. Sara was more of the nice middle class achiever type. Wholesome, vaguely hippyish. She had only two serious boyfriends before me. The first was her high school boyfriend. Dennis. They stayed together for the first two years of college, and after they broke up, they stayed "friends" (I'd met him—a short, mousy guy who played acoustic guitar in coffee shops). She left Dennis for a grad student in her Philosophy department—a self-proclaimed feminist writing a dissertation on Ann Rice. He dumped Sara a year later for his male professor.

I met Sara at a party two years before—in 1998. I was back from six months of wandering around Europe with a backpack and Eurail pass. I had started to hate myself and every other American I saw. And every Spanish and Italian and French and German person. I had only been back in the States for a week, and I was still getting used to the fact that you could take a long hot shower or drink a glass of cold milk or that people could understand me when I spoke to them. So maybe I was overly vulnerable, but Sara just killed me. She was wearing a goofy beret, with her frizzy black hair sticking out around the sides. She was pretty and nice and smart and funny. And American (even in that beret). I don't know. We hit it off. A month later we moved in together.

Two years later and I still felt the same way—she still killed me. But it hadn't worked out. I guess that's all I can say.

I parked in the garage of our building—one of those fancy new apartment buildings with underground parking and security and marble floors and elevators and everything. It was crazy to think that between the two of us we could afford something like this. I had been against the idea, but Sara had been so excited about it that I had to go along. I buzzed Sara to warn her I was on the way up and then I took the elevator up to the eighth floor.

Sara had left the front door ajar. I walked in to see her there with her friend, Beth. They were standing in the living room like they were waiting for me—waiting to get this over with. Sara was wearing jeans and one of her preppy cardigan sweaters. She looked kind of tomboyish compared to Beth, who always wore makeup and form-fitting black outfits.

Beth hated me. She'd hated me since day one. She never laughed at my jokes, and half the time she pretended that she couldn't understand me or didn't even hear me. Sara had announced that Beth was moving in like it was an afterthought, like it had nothing to do with nothing. But I figured it was a package deal: Beth's in, I'm out. So now they were both standing in the middle of the living room, arms crossed, staring at me.

Sara said, "All set?" I know she was trying to sound casual, but her voice was all weird and screechy.

"Yeah," I said.

"Got my keys?"

"Oh," I said. "Right."

I tossed Sara the keys from half-way across the room—harder than I meant to. Sara made a face as they bounced off her shoulder and fell to the floor.

"Nice catch," I said.

Beth glared at me while Sara bent down to pick up the keys. Fuck it. I could be a dick. I was going to be a dick for a while.

I went to get my brother's bike. It was at the end of the hall, leaned up against the wall.

Now, about the bike. This wasn't some little kiddie BMX bike. It was a polished chrome PK Ripper fitted with three piece Cooks Bros cranks and a CNC-machined Tuf-Neck stem. The thing was designed for launching yourself off huge ramps and jumping over picnic tables and riding down long flights of stairs. My brother could do all sorts of sick stuff with this bike—he was like a superhero or some guy in a Mountain Dew commercial. When he went off to college in Oregon, he left it at our parents' house—he was worried that it would be stolen in his dorm, and maybe he had a point, since his college was the only place that had accepted him with his criminal record. Then, when Phil retired a few months before, our folks suddenly sold their Tacoma house and forced me and Nick to clear all our stuff out before they moved up to Port Townsend. Nick asked me to keep the bike for him for a while, and I had been given strict instructions regarding its storage and care. He had called me a few days before to announce that he would be coming up in a week or two to take it back. So I thought I'd use it until he showed up, or until I figured out a better way to get around.

I could hear Sara and Beth talking in low voices in the other room. Well, I was out of there. I got on Nick's bike and literally rode out the door.

Two

You don't know pain until you slam your shin into a bear trap pedal. It will make you puke.

Okay, I didn't puke, but I sure thought about it as I lay there, clutching my leg. Lamely, I'd tried to bunny hop off the curb. But my shoes were wet from the rain and my foot slipped off the pedal. The cranks swung around and whack! I dumped the bike and collapsed onto the wet pavement.

When I pulled up my pant leg, there were big raised welts on my shin—white and vaguely bluish at first, but soon they turned bright red as they swelled with blood. Within a minute blood was running down my shin and into my sock.

I managed to get back on the bike, feeling shaky, my mouth suddenly dry. I hit warp speed as I rode down the narrow walkway on the Ballard bridge. My fingers hurt from the cold and my nose was running. Then, as soon as the road flattened out and started climbing a bit—past the Walgreens and the new Safeway—I ran out of wind and my lungs started to hurt. The seat was so low that I had to stand up to pedal. When I sat down to coast the bike would lose speed almost immediately. I probably needed to get some air in the tires.

When I finally got back to the house, Dan was sitting on the couch with two girls, watching TV. One was Tammy, his girlfriend. The other—who turned out to be Tammy's new friend Kelly—I hadn't seen before.

The first thing I thought when I saw Kelly was that I wanted to fuck her. This took me somewhat by surprise—only a small percentage of women aroused much of anything in me, and usually, it built up more slowly. With Kelly, it was instantaneous. I realized that this was the first thing that had happened since I got dumped by Sara that made being dumped seem not all that bad. Normally, lust would be countered by a vague feeling of guilt and confusion. There was no guilt and confusion here.

"Keith," Dan said. "What's up?"

"Nothing much," I said.

"You all moved in and everything?"

"All moved in."

"Cool," Dan said. "Hey, this is Kelly."

"Hi," I said, trying to be cool, though it's hard to be cool when your ass is wet and your shin is throbbing with pain.

When Kelly said, "Hi," back, I detected an accent. British? German? Hard to tell from just one word, but it was definitely there.

Kelly had short brown hair, pale skin and dark brown eyes. She was wearing a pink Hello Kitty sweatshirt and jeans. Pink socks. She looked like she might be twenty. A twenty-year-old dressed like she was twelve.

Dan said, "So dude, we're going bowling."

"Bowling," I said.

"Yeah, you wanna come?"

"Come on," Tammy said. "It'll be fun."

I liked Tammy. She was cute and spunky. Dan had met her when she brought her mom's car in to have new tires installed at his shop. She was going to community college and still living with her mom. She had just gotten braces and was suddenly embarrassed of her smile.

"Okay," I said. "Just give me a second."

I left the bike in the living room—leaned it up against the wall in the corner—and went down to the basement.

I cleaned up my leg in the industrial sink near the laundry machines, then put on new pants, socks and shoes. I looked at my watch. Seven o'clock. Usually, this time on a Sunday night Sara and I would be cooking dinner, talking about renting a video and maybe going to bed early.

When I got back upstairs, Darryl was there. Dan and the girls were looking at Darryl, and Darryl was looking at my brother's bike.

Darryl was tall—well over six feet—and skinny, but the first thing you noticed about him was his hair: he was in his thirties, but it was already gray. The next thing you noticed was that he didn't smile. He looked angry—or glum, it was hard to tell which.

Darryl turned to me when I walked in. "This your bike?"

"It's my brother's."

He nodded. "Mind if I check it out?"

I shrugged. "Sure."

Darryl got on the bike and did a track stand in the middle of the room. Then, effortlessly, he wheelied up onto the coffee table.

"Alright!" Dan said.

The coffee table was noticeably swaying. Tammy pulled her legs back and said, "Don't fall on me."

Darryl stayed on the table a few seconds longer, rocking back and forth against the front brake. Then he hopped back off the coffee table and stepped off the bike. He said, "Your brother has good taste." He handed the bike back to me and then walked into the kitchen.

No one said anything for a moment. Then Dan said, "We going?"

Suddenly both girls had to go pee. Dan sighed and put on his Minnesota Vikings jacket. He was still a major Vikings fan after all these years. I guess it helped that the Seahawks sucked—I was still a Niners fan. The baggy purple jacket made Dan look even bigger. Dan had been a fat kid when we were in high school, but he'd spent a lot of time in the gym over the last few years and now he was just plain big.

Dan and I stepped outside to wait for the girls. It was getting dark already, and there was a light breeze. Next door, the wind chimes were going full tilt. Those neighbors were new—they had bought the house well over a year ago, but only moved in after a long and extensive renovation. A few weeks before they had set up a satellite dish and installed a hot tub in the backyard. Then they put up the wind chimes. I knew this was a pet peeve with Dan—first he'd had to live with the noise of the renovation, now he had to listen to wind chimes.

Dan was still shaking his head about it when Tammy came outside. "I'm gonna have to do something about those wind chimes," he said.

"Oh, you are not," Tammy said, and punched him in the arm.

"Ow," Dan said. "Jesus."

Dan's Cutlass was parked right in front of the house. Dan had bought the car when we were in high school and had slowly rebuilt everything. He'd put on the finishing touch a few months ago—new silver paint job and polished mag wheels.

Kelly and I climbed in back and sank into the low, vinyl seats. Dan got behind the wheel and Tammy slid across the front bench seat to be right next to him. He fired it up—low burbling noises from the dual exhaust—and we were off.

As we rumbled down the city streets, Kelly and I were both looking straight ahead. I felt like I was in high school again. In fact, Dan and I used to go out with girls in the Cutlass in high school—only, back then, the Cutlass was always stalling out at stoplights, and it leaked so much exhaust into the cabin that we always had to ride with the windows open. I glanced down at Kelly's long legs. Her shoelaces had little hearts on them.

Dan switched on the radio—first a bunch of annoying advertisements for new cars and Caribbean vacations—and when "Pride (In the Name of Love)" by U2 came on, Dan turned it up and started singing along. Dan knew I hated U2. Once, after being totally disillusioned by a concert at the Tacoma Dome, he had helped me skip my U2 records down the street like Frisbees. I tried to catch a copy of "Boy" after throwing it way up into the air and ended up going to the emergency room for stitches.

"Dude," I said. "Turn that shit off."

"What?" Dan said, acting all innocent.

"What?" both girls said.

Here we go, I thought—the Keith and Dan show. I said, "I hate this fucking song."

"How can you say that?" Dan said, and I could see him grinning in the rear-view mirror. "It's about Martin Luther King."

"I don't give a shit," I said. "This song sucks."

Dan said, "What are you, a communist?"

"I love this song," Tammy said.

Dan turned it up even louder and kept singing, "In the name of love..."

"Asshole," I said.

Kelly giggled.

We went and got dinner over at Dick's burgers. The place was supposed to be a 50's throwback and it was a big hangout—especially on weekends. I think Dan liked going there because it was the kind of place where people noticed the Cutlass.

The rain had stopped and it had turned into something of a nice evening. We all leaned against the car and ate our burgers.

Kelly was the only person who didn't get a burger. Instead, she got a shake and some fries.

"Aren't you guys scared about mad cow disease?" she said.

"No," Dan said.

"Well, I am," Kelly said. She stuck a few more fries in her mouth. She had short nails with chipped red nail polish.

"We have higher standards over here," Dan said. "It's you fucking Europeans who have all the problems."

"Where are you from?" I said to Kelly.

Kelly didn't answer me. She was smirking at Dan. "Right," she said. "You don't even know where that burger came from. It's probably a cow from Argentina or New Zealand."

"Mmmmmm. New Zealand cow," Dan said. "My favorite."

"Do you even know what causes mad cow disease?" Kelly said.

"They got it from sheep or something," Dan said.

Kelly shook her head. "Cannibalism," she said. "The poor cows are forced to eat other cows."

"That's gross," Tammy said.

Kelly nodded. "They grind up dead cow parts and mix it into their food."

"Protein," Dan said, taking another bite of his burger.

Tammy said, "Can we talk about something else?"

"Like what?" Dan said.

"I don't know," Tammy said. "Something that isn't gross?"

"Oh, I forgot to tell you!" Kelly said. "Yesterday this huge bird shit on my head."

"Gross!" Tammy said.

"It took me like an hour to get it all out. There were big chunks." Kelly laughed and a fry shot out of her mouth.

"Yeah, well I knew a girl who had a bird shit in her mouth," Dan said.

"Bullshit," I said, laughing.

"It's true," Dan said. "She was looking up at the sky and this huge bird shit landed right on her face and some went into her mouth. She was freaking—spitting and crying and stuff. It was nuts."

"You guys!" Tammy said. "Stop it!"

"Yeah? Well check this out," I said. I pulled up my pant leg and showed them my shin. It was all purple and welted and there was a nice scab forming.

"Dude," Dan said. "What'd you do?"

"Fucking smacked it on the pedal of my brother's bike."

"That's really sick," Kelly said.

"I think you have mad shin disease," Dan said.

Dan and Kelly were laughing. Tammy went and threw her burger in the trash.

We had to wait around for a lane at the bowling alley. Tammy complained that her bowling shoes were too small—that they were cutting into her heel. She traded them in for ones the next size up and then complained that they were too large. She walked around in them like she was a duck, like she was wearing clown shoes. Meanwhile, Dan went and got a bunch of Budweisers in bottles shaped like bowling pins.

While all this was going on, I learned that Kelly was a nanny, that she was here on a temporary visa from Sweden. Stockholm to be exact.

"Wow," I said.

"Wow?" she said. "Why do you say wow?"

"I don't know." Then I said, "You don't look Swedish."

"My mother is from Spain."

"You don't sound Swedish, either. You sound British or something."

"I did some schooling in England."

"Schooling?" I said, and laughed.

"What? It's not a word?"

"No, it's a word," I said.

"Then why did you laugh?" She looked all hurt—kind of pouty.

"Sorry," I said. Then I said, "So why'd you come to Seattle?"

"I thought it would be fun."

"Is it?"

She shrugged. "It's okay."

"Hey losers," Dan said, "We got a lane."

Kelly killed us all at bowling. She didn't have the right form or anything, and she almost always dropped the ball—with a loud crash that would make the serious bowler guys in the next lane turn and look at us. But she almost always got a spare, and she got quite a few strikes, too.

"Damn, how'd you get so good?" I said after she did another super low speed strike—the pins just kind of falling over one by one.

"The kids like bowling," she said. The kids were the kids in the family she was living with. Turns out she had done a lot of bowling since she had come to Seattle.

Meanwhile, Dan and I bowled a whole series of fast, hard gutter balls. I have to say there is something strangely satisfying about a gutter ball—the hard slap of the ball against the backboard, all ten pins lifting in the air as the bar sweeps cleanly underneath.

Before we knew it we'd played about four games.

"I hate these new computerized scoring systems," Dan said.

"Yeah," Tammy said. "You can't cheat."

"We better quit while we still have some money," Dan said.

When the girls went off to the bathroom, Dan said, "You should go for it."

"You think?"

"Man, I would. You're a free man." Then he said, "Just don't get her drunk. She gets kinda weird."

"How so?"

"She gets really emotional."

"What? Like crying and stuff?"

"Dude," he said, nodding. He took a long drink from his beer. Then he said, "Also, she has this weird rodent for a pet. A ferret or something. Usually she brings it with her."

"So how does Tammy know her?"

"They've been taking this African dance class together."

"Huh," I said.

"I'm telling you, man. Go for it."

Later, we dropped Kelly off at a huge house in Montlake. As soon as we pulled up, Tammy said, "I've got to pee."

"You can hold it," Dan said.

"No I can't!"

"Okay, okay," Kelly said. "Just promise to be very quiet."

"What about us?" Dan said.

"You stay here," Tammy said.

"Yeah, we'll stay here," I said.

The girls ran up the front walk and went into the house. Dan and I got out of the car.

"Check out this house," Dan said.

"Big."

"Yeah."

The house was imposing and ostentatious and ugly all at the same time. There was a circular driveway with a Lexus and a Land Rover parked out front.

"Kelly said he's a major asshole."

"Who?"

"The guy who owns the house."

"Oh, right."

Dan looked around. "I'm just waiting for someone to call the cops on us." Dan hated cops. It was a thing with him. Then he said, "So what's your plan?"

"Plan?"

"You know. Now that you're out of the bitch's house."

"Don't call her a bitch," I said.

"Whatever. So what's the plan?"

"No plan."

"Just chillin'?"

"I guess."

"You should be happy."

"You think?"

"Yeah, fuck Sara."

"Yeah."

"I guess you did."

"Good one," I said.

"Hey, you don't have a car, do you?"

"Nope."

"Gotta have a car."

I shrugged.

"There's a guy at work who's selling his car. If you don't want the stereo, I bet he'd sell it to you cheap."

"How cheap?"

"Like real cheap."

"What kind of car?"

"A Celica. Has some rust but otherwise it's not bad."

I laughed. "You're the guy who's always talking shit about Japanese cars."

"Yeah, but they don't break. Plus, you're broke and clueless."

"True," I said. Dan had helped me buy my Dart, and he had done most of the work on it. I think he was more upset than I was when it got totaled.

"I'm telling you," Dan said. "Just hang out with me and you'll have a new car and a new girlfriend in no time."

"Sounds good," I said.

Tammy came running out of the house. She was skipping and flapping her arms like a bird. She ran up and punched Dan in the arm.

"Ow. What was that for?"

"Nothing," Tammy said.

In the car, Tammy turned around in the seat and said, "Kelly really likes you."

"Oh," I said.

"Oh," Tammy said, mocking me.

I shrugged.

"You're blushing," Tammy said.

"No I'm not."

"Yeah you are."

"It's dark," I said. "How do you know?"

She turned on the dome light and squealed. "Yes you are!"

Dan glanced in the rear-view mirror. "You are, dude."

"That's so cute!" Tammy said.

Back at Dan's house, we were greeted by the sound of wind chimes, tinkling in the wind.

Dan started shaking his head. "That's it," he said.

"Don't," Tammy said.

She grabbed at Dan's arm but he pulled away. He walked up to the neighbor's front porch. It took him a minute to unhitch the wind chime. It made a ton of noise.

"Oh shit," Tammy said. She put her hand over her mouth, trying not to laugh.

We saw a light come on in the back of the house.

"Dan!" Tammy said.

Dan ran across the yard and we all ran into the house. We were all laughing.

"Do you think they saw?" Tammy said.

"No," Dan said.

We peeked out the kitchen window at the house next door. After a moment, the light went back off.

Dan handed me the wind chime. "Here, it's a present for you."

"Thanks," I said.

"Hey, no problem." Dan yawned. "Well, I'm going to bed. You all set downstairs?"

"Yeah," I said.

"Where are you sleeping?" Tammy said.

"On the floor I guess."

She made a sad face. "Poor Keith."

"He's tough," Dan said. "He can handle it."

I nodded. "I can handle it."

"See?" Dan said, poking Tammy in the side.

"Alright." She smiled at me, her braces flashing. "Pleasant dreams."

I didn't realize how tired I was until I got downstairs and started getting ready for bed. It was all I could do to shove the cables and pedals out of the way, spread out my sleeping bag and set my alarm for work.

Three

Work. What can I say about work except that it sucked? I hadn't really thought about it all weekend, and then I woke up late and in a rush for the bus. But once I got on the bus (a new bus but it was the same as my old bus) and started looking down on all the other poor schmucks on their morning commute, I knew I was going to quit. I'd been thinking about it for months, and now that I wasn't living with Sara anymore, now that I wouldn't be expected to keep up with her level of spending, well, why put up with it any longer? I got off the bus feeling determined. And when I stepped out of the elevator, I had that Twisted Sister song in my head—"We're Not Gonna Take It!"

I pulled open the glass door with BONNER TECHNOL-OGIES written across it in big white block lettering. Everyone who worked there called it boner. The cute blonde receptionist had recently gotten her nose pierced. Now it was infected—inflamed with some pus—and she was dabbing at it with a cotton ball. I smiled at her and headed down the carpeted hallway and into the maze of cubicles.

The whole cubicle lifestyle blows—the windowless, ergonomically correct, fluorescent lighting, beige lifestyle. Sit around and play video games. Decorate your cube with mountain bike calendars, model cars, snow globes, photos of babies, parents, pets, graduation day. Pick your beverage—purified water in a big plastic water bottle, gourmet coffee in a stainless-steel thermos, or Diet Coke. Choose a screensaver that says something about you as an individual.

I sat down in my cheap, half-broken ergonomic swivel chair and fired up the computer. Most of the chairs in our office were broken, and people were always stealing each other's chairs to try to get one that still worked. One guy had even chained his chair to his desk with a bike lock. I'd given up. No one messed with my chair— the pneumatic adjuster was blown, so it was kind of a low rider.

My computer was slow. It hadn't been behaving well for about a month now. I'd had one of the tech support guys mess with it the week before but he had only made it worse. Whatever. Didn't matter now. I figured I'd erase everything on my hard drive. Force my hand. Pretend I never existed.

I'd had this particular job for a little less than a year. Bonner was a software company that made an obscure and highly specialized product that I didn't really under-stand. I didn't need to understand it, though—that wasn't my job.

I'm not even going to try to describe what exactly I did. I'd been explaining it to my parents and people at parties for the last two years, and frankly it didn't make a whole lot of sense. And the more accurately I described what I did, the more it sounded like total fucking bullshit.

It was stupid and useless and I knew it. Still, people were willing to pay me good money to do it. Weird.

This was my third job in the last two years. I usually moved on when the politics got to be too much for me, or when my other friends quit, or when I got bored, or when I thought I could get more money somewhere else. Changing jobs was a rush. But then once you settled into a new job, it was the same old shit. Same politics, same stupid deadlines, same coffee and bagels and watching the clock.

But beyond all this sameness, there was always something unique about each job. It usually had nothing to do with the job itself. It was the X Factor. Something seemingly small could have a big impact on the work environment. Usually, after I left a job I'd forget the work and the politics and most of the people and just remember the X Factor.

At my first real job out of college, X Factor was asbestos. It was discovered in the building a few months after I started there. We kept being moved around the building as the asbestos team came in, sealed off the floor, and did whatever they did—all I know is that it involved full-body suits and huge sheets of plastic. When we finally got back to our original office, the whole atmosphere seemed different. It seemed too clean or something. People tried to redecorate but it wasn't the same. A few people left and some new ones started, and it was like a whole new company. I bailed after a year.

At my last job the X Factor was internet porn. The company was pretty much all guys, and it seemed like the only thing people did there was look at porn. There was a running contest to see who could find the sickest, most depraved shit. It was kind of funny for a day or two, but then I realized how lame and miserable everyone was. I eventually left that job after a few months because my boss was an asshole, but what I remember most is seeing four losers crowded around someone's cubicle, laughing self-consciously with their hands in their pockets.

The X Factor at this job was the bathroom. Our company shared a floor—and therefore the bathroom—with a company on the other side. No one really knew what they did at that company. All we knew was that it was made up of men in their late fifties. Those guys had problems. If you've seen the movie *Glengarry Glen Ross*, you know what I'm talking about. But it wasn't just that. There was a problem with low water pressure in the building. There definitely was a problem with flushing, with overflowing, with foul odors. A tile floor covered with wet footprints and half-dissolved toilet paper was not the kind of thing you want to see first thing in the morning.

A simple trip to the bathroom was something to dread, something to worry about. People would say, "You been to the bathroom lately?" and just kind of bug their eyes out at you. On a really bad day, the stench and possibly a really scary image would follow you back to your cubicle. It was truly disturbing.

A woman named Diane sat at the cube next to me. I didn't really know what she did—I'd never asked. She was always typing stuff into Excel spreadsheets, and she had wrist braces on each arm.

Carpal tunnel was contagious. Diane was one of the first to get it. It swept through the whole office like the plague. I started feeling like I had it (even though I made a concerted effort to not type or really do much of anything). A few months before, the company hired an ergonomic specialist to come through and do all these measurements. We were all supposed to do these exercises now. Make sure your monitor was at the right height, your keyboard at the right angle. Sit up straight, don't slump. Eat your vegetables.

I could hear Diane typing away as I happily deleted everything on my hard drive. I loved dragging stuff to the trash. Are you sure you want to delete LogFile.htm? Hell yes.

And then Don walked up. He was one of the marketing guys that I had to deal with sometimes. I liked Don, but he was still annoying. He always wore these goofy Hawaiian shirts, and he was one of the few people who seemed oblivious to the whole bathroom scenario. The guy was always in there—brushing his teeth, shaving, reading the paper in the stall. And he liked to talk to you while you were in there. You'd be taking a shit and he'd ask you about your weekend (I guess he'd recognize my Adidas or something).

Don looked over my shoulder as I pulled more stuff to the trash.

"Good weekend?"

"Yeah," I said, automatically. But then wondered what a "bad" weekend would be.

"Doing a little spring cleaning?"

"Uh huh."

"Remember we have a meeting at two."

"I don't think I'm gonna make it."

"Why?"

"I'm gonna quit today."

"Really?" Don looked half sad, half pleased to get some good gossip.

"Don't tell anyone, okay?"

"I won't. I promise."

"Thanks."

He walked away. Half the company would know in ten minutes. The only person that wouldn't was my boss, Mindy. No one talked to her if they could avoid it.

When I finished deleting pretty much everything, I walked over to say hello to Sam and Cathleen—two of my work friends (work friends meant you did lunch from time to time, included each other in stupid group email lists and hung out together at the occasional work party). Cathleen was sitting on Sam's desk. They had a little office romance going. It was cute.

Sam said, "Dude, I hear you're quitting."

"Yup," I said.

"Really?" Cathleen said. "You're leaving us?"

"I'm leaving you."

Cathleen slid off Sam's desk and put her arm around me—like we were in a chorus line, like we were gonna do a little dance.

"I can't believe you're leaving us," she said.

"I'm sorry," I said.

"It's okay," she said. She kicked out a foot and said, "You like my shoes?" She was wearing red combat boots.

"Yeah," I said.

"You really gonna quit?" Sam said.

"Yup," I said.

"Sweet." He gave me a high five.

I went to the kitchen to get a Coke out of the fridge. This was one of the main perks at this company—free Cokes. I wanted my last Coke.

As usual, several people were sitting around the large Formica table. I'd never made an effort with any of these people, never bothered to learn anyone's name. I had my little private code names for each of them, though. Big Lady (well, she was big—she looked like John Goodman doing Janet Reno on Saturday Night Live) was microwaving leftover Thai food—or that's what it smelled like, anyway. Sweater Guy was drinking some tea (I think he was a programmer, and he always wore the same brown sweater). And The Sisters (two women who worked in accounting—I wasn't sure if they were actually sisters, but they sure looked similar) were paging through a clothing catalog.

No one paid any attention to me, either (I wondered what kind of private code names people had for me). I got my Coke out of the fridge and then I went to go see Mindy.

When Mindy first interviewed me, I had actually liked her. She seemed tough and professional and no bullshit. I thought we understood each other, but a few days into my first week I started getting a weird vibe. I think maybe I was a disappointment (which I can understand) but it was like she took it personally—perhaps because she couldn't blame me on anyone but herself. She took any excuse to humiliate me at meetings or in front of other people. I always took it pretty well—I'd just smile—and I think that made her hate me more. I could say a lot more about Mindy, but what's the point, really? She was the kind of person that you could really fixate on, but at the same time, she'd be easy to forget after I was out of there.

Mindy was on the phone when I walked in. She wore the worst clothes. Weird frilly crochet dresses with white aerobics shoes. When she interviewed me, she had been dressed up in her airline stewardess costume that she wore on days when she had meetings with clients.

She glared at me when I walked in but then went back to her conversation. I sat down in the leather seat facing her and waited. At first I thought that she was in the middle of some sort of important business call—not that I cared, really—but then I realized that it was about her Volvo. It was in the shop.

She hung up.

"Yes Sam."

"Keith," I said. I don't know why, but she got the two of us confused.

She looked bored. "I'm sorry, Keith. What can I do for you?"

"I quit."

She looked at me for a moment. "Just like that?"

"Yup."

"I see. Are you planning to give us two weeks?"

I thought about it for a moment—or I pretended to. Then I said, "Nope."

"I'm sorry to hear that."

I shrugged.

"Well, it was nice working with you." She stood up and put out her hand.

What the hell? I didn't know what else to do, so I shook her hand. "Likewise," I said.

She sat back down and said, "What's a master cylinder?"

"What?"

"A master cylinder. That's what's wrong with my car."

"I think it has something to do with the brakes."

"Oh," she said. "Right. Thanks." Then she went back to work.

Last stop was the bookkeeping lady—Sharon. I wanted to see if she could speed up my last check.

Sharon looked like my grandmother. But she was way tougher. She shook her head. "No can do."

"Oh please, pretty please?"

She smiled. "I'm sorry. We'll mail it to you."

"Okay. I have a new address..."

That was it. It was simple really. I went back to my desk but there was nothing more to do. Of course, there was the temptation to try to pull off some sort of parting shot—perhaps a small act of sabotage. But that required too much imagination (not to mention talent). I didn't even have the energy to send around a farewell email. So I went over to the supply room and loaded up on Post-It notes and my favorite Uni-Ball pens, grabbed another Coke from the kitchen and then I got the hell out of there.

Four

The first thing I noticed when I got back to the house was that the bike was missing. For a second, I thought that maybe someone had moved it, but I took a quick look around—in the kitchen, upstairs and downstairs—and it was definitely gone. Son of a bitch.

I couldn't remember when I had seen it last. Had it been there when we got back from bowling? Had it been there in the morning before work?

The only guy home was Ken. He was out back messing around with his compost bins. Ken was a compost Nazi. He made Dan and Darryl separate everything out into various categories. Vegetables in one bin. Fruits (non-citrus) in another. Everything else in a third bin. And they had to buy non-food items that would compost well. For example, they had to buy paper towels without bleach—bleach messed up the compost.

I went outside to see if Ken knew anything about the bike. He was standing over by the back fence, staring at his hand. When I got closer, I saw that he was having some kind of larva problem with one of the compost bins. There were scary black bugs everywhere—like a science experiment gone wrong. And then I realized that he was holding one of the bugs in his open palm. He brought it up close to his face and nudged it gently with his finger. It appeared that he was talking to it—whispering sweet nothings into the bug's ear.

"Hey Ken," I said.

Ken looked up at me. He was doing the whole grad student look—the John Lennon glasses and army jacket and goofy brown leather shoes. At first it seemed like he had no idea who I was, but then he said, "Yeah?"

"Hey," I said. "You seen my bike?"

He said, "What bike?"

The bug made a break for it. It started running down Ken's arm. Ken stopped its progress with his hand, then bent down and released the bug onto the ground.

I said, "Have you seen Darryl?"

"No."

"Okay, thanks." Then I said, "Everything under control?"

"Yeah," Ken said. "Why?"

"No reason," I said.

I went back inside and started pacing around. Shit. Shit. Shit. Shit.

It had to be fucking Darryl. Or maybe Dan was fucking with me. I bet that was it. I called Dan at work.

Dan worked at Big Bob's Tires. He was a tire guy. I could hear the air guns in the background.

"Hey Dan," I said.

"Keith," he said. "What's up?"

"You seen my bike?"

"Your bike?"

"My brother's PK Ripper."

"No. Why?"

"It's not here."

"I'm sure it's around somewhere."

"It's not. I checked."

"Maybe Darryl has it."

"That's what I was thinking."

"Yeah man, don't worry. He's probably riding it around or something."

"Fucking pisses me off."

Then Dan said, "Hey, I talked to Carl."

"Who's Carl?"

"The dude with the Celica. He'd said he'd sell it to you for five hundred without the stereo."

"Yeah?"

"Yeah, but you better come do it today. He needs the money now. Otherwise he's gonna take it down to some lot and just take what they give him for it."

"I don't know."

"Dude. You need a car." He laughed. "You don't even have a bike."

"That's not funny."

Then he said, "Hey, shouldn't you be at work?"

"Yeah. But I quit."

"Hey congrats. That's awesome." I heard some yelling in the background, then a crash. "Shit, I gotta go. But come over here and check out that car. Seriously."

I did need a car. But this seemed kind of rushed. Plus, I was still freaking about the bike.

I'd had my bike stolen when I was ten—when we were

still living in California. I had been crazy about that bike—a chrome Mongoose with mag wheels—and had ridden it everywhere. Then one day I left it locked up outside the local arcade while I played Defender and Galaga. When I came out, the lock was lying there, cut in half. I'll never forget that feeling—it was way worse than when my Dart got totaled. But this wasn't about me—it wasn't about my feelings. It was about Nick. I knew my brother wouldn't take it too well.

Maybe I need to explain more about my brother. He was nineteen, in the middle of his first year of college. He was a bit of a miscreant. Over the years, he had been busted for shoplifting, grand theft auto, various moving violations, small scale drug dealing and one fairly bad beating outside a 7-11 that had made the local newspapers (to be fair, the guy he beat up was older and bigger, and had started the fight—my brother, as they say, finished it). And those are just the things for which he'd been caught. He'd done some time in juvenile detention and he'd done a lot of community service. In other words, he was a fuck up.

The thing is, if you knew him, all of this seemed kind of funny. For the most part he was a reasonable, intelligent guy with a good sense of humor. He just had something of a quick temper and a bit of a wild side. He also had guns.

I'm not a child psychologist, not a psychoanalyst, but I think that all of this stemmed from the fact that Nick hated Phil (his real dad, my stepdad). I'd gotten off relatively easy with Phil—I wasn't his kid, and I'd been the one he needed to impress to score my mom. But for some reason, Phil had always been hard on Nick. Our mom spoiled the crap out of Nick—he was the baby, after all. But Phil came down hard on him.

The other part of the problem was Nick's friend Tony. Tony was a bad influence. He was getting to be something of a big-time amphetamine dealer and had made Nick his partner. I think the only reason Nick agreed to go to college was because it would give them a whole new market.

Anyway, if the bike really was gone, I wasn't worried about what my brother would do to me—we got along great, had never had a fight (part of this had to do with the six years between us—might have been a different story if we were closer in age). No, I was worried what he'd do in a more general, loose cannon sense. Or what he and Tony would do. As that guy outside the 7-11 had discovered the hard way, it didn't take much to set my brother off.

I went downstairs to my room and tried to relax. But it wasn't exactly cool hanging out in a smelly, windowless room with a bunch of band equipment. So I went back upstairs.

The second I sat down on the couch, Ken walked in. He was mixing some nasty looking plant food in a large Pyrex measuring cup. When he saw me, he said, "Hey, do you think you could help me with something?"

To be honest, Ken freaked me out. I said, "Um, actually, I have to go somewhere right now."

"Oh, okay." He looked hurt.

I smiled, then walked out the front door. I guess I was gonna go get that car.

It was a long walk to Dan's work. I probably could've taken the bus, but I wasn't in a hurry. Hey, I had all the time in the world!

It was funny to think that everyone was still at the office—Sam, Cathleen, Sharon, Mindy, Don—going about their day without me. I used to get the same feeling when I was a kid and stayed home sick. It made me happy but it also felt weird.

I stopped at the bank on the way to Dan's work and took out five hundred dollars.

My account balance wasn't looking all too healthy—hard to believe, really, considering how much money I had been making over the last two years. And there was a rather large Visa bill looming in the not-so-distant future. Shit.

Those guys at Dan's work had fun. They wore ear plugs and eye protection and fucked around—bowling tires at each other and shooting each other with compressed air. Dan had worked there for a few years now. The pay wasn't too bad, and other than the occasional drug test, they treated him pretty well.

When I walked into the garage, Dan was at the bead breaker, prying a tire off the rim. He glanced back and nodded at me. It was funny—he was actually pretty serious about his job. I stepped back outside. It had started raining again so I waited under the overhang.

Dan came out a few minutes later. We walked over to his Cutlass and got inside.

"What's up?" Dan said.

"Not much," I said.

Dan let out a fart.

"Nice," I said. I rolled down my window.

"Can't believe you quit. We got to celebrate."

Dan pulled out his rolling paper and started rolling a joint.

"I thought you guys had to piss in a cup."

"Just did. Won't have to for another three months."

Dan finished rolling the joint, licked it, then lit it up. He took a long drag and then passed me the joint.

I took a hit, then exhaled. "So where's Carl?"

"I told him you were here. He's gonna drive around with the car."

"Cool."

Dan was just nodding and smiling at me.

"What?" I said.

"It's the new Keith."

"What do you mean?"

He laughed. "Ditched your girlfriend, quit your job. You're a fucking rebel, man!"

"Yeah," I said. "That's me."

Dan shook his head. "I love it."

And then the Celica pulled up.

"Holy shit," I said.

Dan laughed. "It's not as bad as it looks."

I remember from a freshman English class that Flannery O'Connor's hero Hazel Motes had driven a "high, rat-colored" car. Well, the Celica was a low, rat-colored car—it was lowered, had some cheap-looking mag wheels, and had once been painted yellow. But the yellow was hard to see now—the car was literally covered with big patches of rust.

Dan and I got out of the Cutlass. I shook Carl's hand. He was a pale, skinny guy with a thin little mustache. He was wearing scratched-up aviator glasses.

I looked at the car again. "I don't know," I said.

"You want to take it for a spin?" Carl said.

And that's when I noticed that the front passenger seat was missing. "Where's the front seat?"

Carl shrugged. "It was that way when I got it."

"And you want five hundred for this?"

"Hey, the wheels are worth more than five hundred."

Dan said, "Dude, it'll be fine. Carl's cool. He put some work into this thing." Then he said, "Where else are you going to find a car so cheap?"

"Yeah, man," Carl said. "The car runs great. It's got new brakes, new shocks, new tires. I know it doesn't look great, but you won't have any problems with it."

"No?"

"No man, it's cool."

"How 'bout three hundred?" I said.

"Four hundred and it's yours," he said.

"Alright," I said.

"Alright!" Carl said. He smiled.

"Do you have to pull the stereo out or something?"

"Already did that. Which reminds me. I left in the main unit cause it's broken. Also, it's kind of boobytrapped."

"What do you mean?"

"Well, when I put it in, I lined the back with razor blades. Someone tries to take it out and they're gonna lose a finger."

"Oh, great," I said. I looked at Dan. Dan was just laughing.

The car did drive fine. Since it was lowered, it felt pretty solid, pretty stealthy. There were big holes in the door panels where the speakers had been, and it needed a new muffler—it was kind of boomy. And not having another seat up front was weird. Still, I liked it better than Sara's fucking Civic. This car had attitude.

A few days before I had been a guy with a girlfriend, a guy with a respectable job, a guy who drove around in a new Honda Civic tuned to NPR. Now I was single, unemployed, driving around in a lowered, beat-to-shit Celica. I liked it.

Five

Darryl got home later that afternoon. I was waiting for him when he walked in the door.

"Hey Darryl," I said. "You don't happen to know where my bike is, do you?" I could just see myself—nervous, with a geeky, nasally voice. Jesus.

Darryl just looked at me for a moment. "No," he said, casually—too casually, I thought. "Why?" And that's when I noticed he cut his lip. Also, his hand was bandaged.

My heart rate was picking up. "Cause it's missing, that's why."

"Huh."

"Did you borrow it?"

"No."

"Well, it's gone."

Darryl said, "So what are you saying?"

"I'm saying it's not here. I talked to Ken and Dan and they haven't seen it either."

"You sure you didn't do something with it?"

"Of course I'm sure."

"Well don't look at me."

With that, he walked past me. Was he limping? I turned and followed him to his room.

"So you think someone broke in and stole it?" I said.

"Beats me." He closed the door in my face.

Like I said before, rule number one for living in the house was don't rock the boat with Darryl. Still, I was pretty sure Darryl had taken the bike. I wasn't going to let him get away with it that easily.

I knocked on the door. No response. I knocked again.

"What?" Darryl said from behind the door.

"I want to talk to you," I said.

The door opened. Darryl was naked except for some not-so-white tighty whities. Now that he was facing me, I couldn't think of anything to say. I tried to see past him—tried to see if the bike was in his room.

He just glared at me for a moment. Then he slammed the door.

Dan got home about an hour after my confrontation with Darryl. I was still kind of shaky. Darryl hadn't emerged from his room.

Dan was in a good mood. "Dude, did you see that total piece of shit parked out in front of the house? I wonder what kind of idiot would drive a car like that."

"Funny," I said.

"Hey, Tammy called me at work. She wants us to go over there. Kelly is gonna come over, too."

"Sounds okay to me," I said.

"Cool. We can take your car." He smiled. "Cruise in style."

Outside, the sky was looking vaguely apocalyptic. Black clouds threatened in the distance, with layers of dull gray and fluffy white turning pinkish red as the sun started to set.

Dan called out "Shotgun," and started laughing. "Oh, whoops, I forgot. I guess I'll sit in back."

He climbed in back and stretched out his legs.

"Hey, I could get used to this. Lots of legroom. All you need is a mini fridge back here and you'd be set."

After a few blocks, I told him about the little scene with Darryl.

"I wouldn't fuck with him," Dan said.

"Yeah, why not?"

"I just wouldn't fuck with the dude, okay?"

"What? You think he's dangerous?"

"No." Then he said, "Well, I don't think so anyway."

"So what's up with the scraped-up lip and the band-aged wrist?"

"Who knows."

"You know that Nick is gonna freak."

"Don't worry. I'm sure the bike will turn up."

Tammy's mom was out of town—off to a big Renaissance festival down in California. She traveled all over the country for these things, dressing up like a court jester and putting on puppet shows. Their house was decorated accordingly— new age bed and breakfast meets the Lord of the Rings. My favorite was the little porcelain gnome collection on the living room mantelpiece. Dan liked to arrange them in obscene positions, which always pissed Tammy off.

Kelly was stuck eating dinner with the kids, so we ordered pizza. After the pizza guy came, Dan said, "Hey

Keith, I bet the Celica would look pretty good with one of those Domino's signs on the roof."

"Yeah, so would the Cutlass."

"Damn," Dan said. "Touchy."

After we finished the pizza, Tammy called Kelly. They talked for a while, and Tammy kept giggling. When she finally got off the phone, she said, "Hey, Kelly needs someone to go pick her up."

They both looked at me.

"I'll go," I said.

I pulled the Celica into the circular driveway and parked it behind the Lexus. A woman in a pink warm-up suit was walking by with a tiny dog in a sweater. She stared at me as I got out of the car. I stared back, then went and rang the doorbell.

Right away, some fat guy answered the door.

"You here for Kelly?"

"Yeah," I said.

He smiled, then winked at me. "This way," he said.

I followed him down a long hallway. Big ass, wrinkled dress shirt tucked in loosely, Topsiders with no socks. When we entered a kitchen the size of a gymnasium, he turned and said, "I'm Bob by the way."

"Keith."

"Well, Keith, make yourself comfortable. I think she's getting dressed."

"Okay." I sat on a chrome stool next to a long marble counter.

Bob passed me a huge wooden bowl filled with potato chips.

"Want some chips?"

"No thanks."

He shrugged, took a handful for himself, then leaned against the counter.

"Kelly is quite something, isn't she?"

"She's nice."

He smiled. "That's one way of putting it."

I didn't know what he meant by that, didn't know how to respond—I didn't even know who this guy was, so I said, "You live here?"

He laughed. "Yeah, this is my house."

"Oh, right."

I was looking around for some sign of the kids that Kelly was supposed to take care of. The place seemed too big and way too clean for kids.

"I saw you pull up," he said. "That's a nice car you got there."

"Thanks."

"They don't make 'em like they used to."

"I guess not."

Bob smiled. He was really gorging on the potato chips. His fingers were getting all greasy. "So what do you do, if you don't mind me asking."

"Uh, nothing at the moment."

"Really? A smart guy like you? In an economy like this?"

"I'm taking some time off."

"Oh, right. That's a good idea. I did that when I was your age. Really helped me focus." Then he said, "I don't know if you're looking for something, but a friend of mine is trying to find someone to work for him."

"Yeah? Doing what?"

"Well, basically live at his house, be around, that kind of thing."

"You mean a personal assistant?"

"Not exactly. Just someone to have around to get the mail, make sure the house doesn't burn down, that kind of thing."

"Huh," I said.

"Just throwing it out there."

"I'll keep it in mind," I said.

At that point, Kelly walked in. Bob said, "Well, here's the prom queen."

Kelly rolled her eyes. I got up and we walked out toward the front door.

"You kids have fun now," he called after us.

"Quite a guy," I said as we closed the door behind us.

"He's a creep," Kelly said. She made a face when she saw the car. "Hey, where's the front seat?"

I didn't see the ferret until we were in the car. She held him up in front of my face while we were waiting at a stoplight.

"I brought Milo with me."

"Hi Milo," I said.

Milo just kind of stared at me with his beady little red eyes. He looked like a long skinny rat. His hair was yellow-ish white. He smelled awful.

"Is he albino?" I said.

"Yes," she said. Then: "What?" She sounded hurt.

I turned around. "Nothing," I said. "He's cute."

She smiled and cuddled him. "He's my little baby."

The first part of the evening was pretty dull. There was nothing on TV so we ended up watching a Civil War documentary on the History Channel.

"What the fuck is this?" Dan said after a while. "This is like a fucking slide show or something. I feel like I'm back in high school."

"They didn't have movie cameras back then," I said.

"They had movie cameras when we were in high school."

"Good one," I said.

"Seriously, how 'bout some re-enactments or something? How hard could that be?"

"That costs money."

"No it doesn't. There are people who live for that kind of shit. You don't even have to pay 'em. Just put an ad in the paper. You'll get a bunch of Civil War junkies calling in sick from their job at the mini mart so they can be in your movie. They'll bring their own costumes and everything."

"What about special effects?"

Dan shrugged. "What's a little dry ice cost?"

I laughed. "Dry ice?"

"Yeah, you know, for the smoke and shit."

"Dude, that's a Kiss concert, not a Civil War movie."

"Same difference," Dan said. "Anyway, why are we watching this? Who cares about all this old shit?"

"You Americans are so funny," Kelly said. "You think anything over a hundred years is old."

"It is old," Dan said.

"No it's not. Rome is old. The Vikings are old."

"The wooly mammoth is old, too," Dan said. "What's your point?"

Kelly just shook her head.

"Hey," Tammy said. "I heard they were going to bring a wooly mammoth back to life."

"Back to life?" Dan said.

"Or take the cells and clone one or something."

"I'd like to see that," Dan said.

Tammy got tired after a while and she and Dan went off to bed early. That left me alone with Kelly. Kelly and Milo.

So then I heard the whole story about Milo. How she had adopted him from some friends of the kids she was taking care of. How he had been neglected as a baby. How the people she lived with hated animals, how they would freak out if they ever learned about him. So poor Milo lived in her closet. She only took him out when it was safe.

It kind of sucked trying to make out with Kelly with the rodent around. I'd try to get my hand up under her shirt and I'd get a handful of fur.

"Don't squish him," she said, giggling.

And when we really started kissing, we had to stop so she could take the gum out of her mouth.

"Where should I put this?" she said.

"I don't know."

But I was really starting to like Kelly. And man, what a body. Finally, she made Milo a nice little bed out of towels on the floor. Milo burrowed.

Later, when I dropped her off at the mansion, she gave me a kiss on the cheek and said, "Milo really likes you."

I had a big stupid smile on my face as I drove home. How many guys could find a new girl just two days after being thrown out by their girlfriend? Not many, I bet. And not many could find anyone like Kelly.

At a stoplight, a Camaro pulled up next to me with AC/DC blaring on the stereo–with Bon Scott belting out, "Touch Too Much."

I started revving the Celica but the guys in the Camaro just laughed at me. When the light turned green, they left me in a cloud of smoke.

Six

It was past midnight by the time I got back to the house. Darryl was at work. His van was gone.

I went into the kitchen to get a glass of water. Ken had set up a grow lamp over some plants he was trying to raise from seeds. There must have been twenty individually labeled pots spread out across the kitchen table. Some of them appeared to be filled with just wet dirt, but others had started to sprout something—little green aliens uncurling in the soft yellow glow.

I knew it was a bad idea, but I wanted to take a look in Darryl's room. I didn't expect to find the bike, but I was hoping to find some sort of clue. Also, I just wanted to look in that fucker's room.

I washed the glass and put it back in the cupboard. Then I walked over to Darryl's room.

On the off chance that Darryl was home, I turned the doorknob very slowly. I half expected it to be locked or booby trapped or alarms to go off or something. But nothing happened. I pushed the door open gently, then switched on the light.

Well, the guy was a neat freak, I can say that much. And something of a minimalist. His bed was made with military precision—it looked like you could bounce a quarter on it. There was a night table and a small bookshelf filled with books. The only other items in the room were a folding chair and a radio sitting on the floor unplugged. There was nothing on the walls, no framed photos of relatives, nothing.

I opened the closet door. Clothes. Shoes. Another folding chair (for guests?). I closed the closet door.

I don't know what I expected—Nazi paraphernalia, weapons, S & M stuff, child pornography. But there was nothing. It was pretty boring. Boring in a scary kind of way.

I looked at the bookshelf. It seemed like he had every Ayn Rand book ever printed, and more than one copy of several of them. I picked up a copy of *The Fountainhead*. Inside, large sections had been underlined.

"Keith?"

I nearly jumped out of my skin. But it was just Ken. He was wearing a ratty-looking bathrobe and glasses. I guess he wore contacts during the day.

I said, "Hi Ken," as casually as I could, but I was shaking.

"What are you doing?" he said.

"Uh..."

"I wouldn't touch his stuff if I was you."

I put the book back on the shelf. Then I walked out of Darryl's room and closed the door behind me.

"Did you see Darryl tonight?"

"Briefly, before he went to work."

"Did he say how he got that cut on his lip?"

"No."

I shook my head.

"Why?" Ken said.

"I think he took my brother's bike."

"You do?"

"Well, someone did. Did you? Did Dan?"

Ken shrugged.

"Fuck," I said.

Ken tightened the sash on his bathrobe and started back to his room. Before he closed his door, he said, "I hope he doesn't notice anything out of order in his room."

I sat on the floor of the basement room and tried to calm down. I was angry at Darryl, angry at Dan for living with Darryl, angry at Sara for kicking me out, angry at my brother for sticking me with his stupid fucking bike, but mostly I was angry at myself. My stomach hurt.

And all of a sudden, I really missed Sara. I wasn't sure if I missed her, exactly, or if I missed not having to deal with this bullshit. And then all sorts of memories started flooding back—cooking dinner together, renting movies, sleeping in, that kind of domestic bliss crap. It was irritating, and I caught myself. Fuck it, I was going to sleep. Everything would seem better in the morning.

***

I woke up to the loudest, most horrible screeching noises you can imagine. It was so close and so loud that at first I thought the noise was coming from me—that it originated from inside my body. But when I finally figured out who I was and where I was, I saw Darryl, standing next to the Marshall stack. He had turned the guitar amp up to ten. One of the guitars was leaning against the speaker, creating the horrible, mind-bending feedback.

Darryl didn't seem to be bothered by the noise, didn't seem to want to stop it. So I did—lunging forward out of my sleeping bag and throwing the switch. The little red light on the amp slowly faded out as the feedback died away. And then I was just sitting there, looking up at Darryl.

He smiled. "Hi asshole."

"Hi," I said. My ears were ringing.

"Listen, next time you go into my room, I will kill you. Do you understand?"

I didn't say anything.

Darryl smiled—it was more like a grimace—and walked to the door. "I want you and all your shit out of here. Now."

Then he walked out of the room.

I was thinking: fucking Ken. Ken you little tattletale shit.

It was as if Darryl had read my mind. He came back into the room. "And next time you decide to snoop around in someone's room, you should turn the light off when you leave."

Of course, I immediately started going back through this scene, trying to figure out how I could have defended myself better—or hell, gone on the attack, accused him of stealing the bike, etc. But I had been soundly defeated and I knew it. What could I do now? It would be impossible to stay under these conditions, and even if I could prove he had stolen the bike, then what? I was fucked. It was time to leave. Game over.

It was a bright, sunny morning. I packed up the Celica with all my stuff. Darryl's bedroom door stayed closed while I did this. The van was parked out front, so I knew he was home. Well fuck him.

When I finished packing, I drove over to Big Bob's Tires.

"That sucks," Dan said.

"You could say that."

We were standing in the waiting room. It smelled like new tires and the burned coffee they provided to customers.

"I told you not to fuck with him," Dan said.

"I'm sure he stole my brother's bike."

"You don't know that."

"Who else do you think did it?"

Dan shrugged. A small child was having a tantrum by the tire counter—throwing himself on the black and white checked linoleum floor and shrieking. His mother tried to ignore him as she talked to the tire salesman.

Dan said, "So now what are you gonna do?"

"I don't know."

"Sorry man," he said. "That really sucks."

"Yup," I said.

Someone yelled Dan's name from the garage.

"I gotta get back to work."

"Okay," I said.

I went back and sat in the Celica. I had half-expected Dan to get angry about Darryl, to defend me, but then

Dan was kind of a kiss ass sometimes—looking out for Number One, for whatever was convenient. Not that I could really blame him. He just liked to play everything cool, stay mellow, stay below the radar.

I started running through my options—there weren't many, and all of them were humiliating. I could call up Sam or Cathleen from work to see if I could stay with them, but I didn't like that idea much. It's one thing to admit failure to close friends, but it seemed desperate to try to lean on work friends. I knew I couldn't stay with Kelly. Tammy's mom was coming back from the Renaissance fair so that was out. So that left Sara or my parents.

Well, I had to go somewhere. I started up the Celica.

I ended up over at Gas Works Park, sitting up on one of the toxic hills. The park had been built on what was once the site of a large gas refinery. The whole place was a biohazard, so they made it into a park. Brilliant. There were areas where they couldn't even get grass to grow.

There was a pretty incredible view of Lake Union, though, and of the city behind it. Sara and I had come out here with a bunch of people on the 4th of July. The place had been crawling with people—it looked like a big ant hill. We pressed ourselves into the crowd, sat down on a picnic blanket and watched the fireworks being launched off a huge old barge.

I went and sat in the exact same spot—this time with almost no one around—and watched people fly kites and walk their dogs. A while after I got there, a truck showed up with Honey Bucket porta potties and people started setting up tents and tables for some kind of event. A high school kid started running a remote-control dune buggy up and down the grass slope. And I just sat there. Picture one of those time lapse movies—people running around at high speed, the sun moving across the sky, and me just sitting there on my ass.

I was thinking I could just get up and leave. Get in the Celica and just drive. Head out across the country. Be like Jack Kerouac. Come to think of it, I had quite a bit in common with Sal Paradise at the beginning of *On the Road*. I had just gotten through a "miserably weary split-up" and was ready for something new. But to tell the truth, I didn't like traveling. I mean, I've traveled enough and it really isn't that interesting—mostly, it's a pain in the ass. I'd rather see the movie.

Of course, I could always go visit my dad in Colorado. I hadn't been out to see him in two years. The last time had been pretty depressing. I mean, I was happy for him in a way—happy that he had followed his dream to be a kayak instructor and everything. But there was something selfish and miserable about his life. He was eating Top Ramen like a college student and living in a small apartment over someone's garage. He was also a hypochondriac, so all he ever talked about were his various ailments.

So I knew I wasn't going anywhere. I was going to sit and wait for Sara to get back from work. Then I was going to go back to the apartment and ask her to let me stay for a little bit longer, until I got things sorted out.

Was this a bad plan? Yes. Did I have a better plan? No. There was also my parents, but that was my backup plan. Emergency only.

So I waited until 6 o'clock—the sun was just starting to set over the city—and then I waited some more. Finally, when I couldn't stand it much longer, I went and got myself a taco at Mr. Taco (I'm sorry, but white people should not be allowed to make Mexican food—especially white people who play in metal bands and wear all black). Then I went over to Sara's.

Sara was pretty surprised to see me, but she let me in. Luckily, Beth wasn't around. We went into the living room and she offered to make me some tea. She had never offered to make me tea before. I said, "Sure, sounds great."

While she was making the tea I looked around. It had only been two days, but they'd completely re-done the place. There was a new white rug on the floor and several Matisse prints on the walls. And there were more plants.

Sara brought in the tea and sat across from me on the couch. It was our same old couch, but they had added some kind of Ecuadorian (or was it Indian?) throw. I played absentmindedly with the little orange tassels.

Sara smiled. She seemed to be waiting for me to say something.

"So," I said. "How's life?"

"Oh, I'm doing okay. How are you?"

"Great," I said.

She was still wearing her work clothes and she looked very professional. She also looked very calm, very collected. She could be a therapist.

"Keith," she said. "Why are you here?"

"I had a bad day," I said.

"What happened?"

After I finished telling her about the bike and Darryl and everything, she seemed to think for a moment, and then she said, "I hope you're not planning to stay here."

I swallowed. "Just for a little while?"

"Keith..."

And that's when I heard the key in the lock. Shit. It was Beth. I was fucked.

Beth walked in wearing her black Gestapo work outfit. Her peach lip gloss matched her fingernail polish. As soon as she saw me, she looked at Sara and said, "Should I go away for a bit?"

"Why?" Sara said. "This is your apartment, too."

This is it, I thought—I'd hit rock bottom. I stood up.

"I gotta go," I said.

Sara looked surprised. She said, "Where are you going to go?"

I wanted to say, "Like you care." But that was too pathetic, too dramatic. Instead, I said, "Home."

Seven

After driving the Celica onto the ferry, I went upstairs and called my parents—I thought I'd better warn them I was coming. My mom answered. She sounded surprised and vaguely concerned—it was the middle of the week after all, and didn't I need to go to work? So I told her I'd quit my job. I didn't tell her about the breakup with Sara. They liked Sara and I knew they wouldn't take it too well.

I'd forgotten that my parents were getting ready to leave for a big trip to Tibet. Seems like the day Phil retired they went nuts. They moved to Port Townsend and then started planning trips everywhere. Phil had read all the Mount Everest books that had been coming out, and so now they were jumping on the Tibet bandwagon. Hey, good for them.

After I hung up I bought a candy bar and went out to the front deck. It was windy and cold out there and I was alone. Just lots of black sky and blackish water running under the ship. By chance, the Celica was right at the front of the ferry, which was open except for a piece of orange netting. One of the ferry guys had put the little wood blocks under the front wheels so it wouldn't launch itself overboard. The Celica appeared to be leading the charge across the Sound, rocking up and down in rhythm with the motion of the boat.

I was trying really hard not to think the poor little old me thoughts, which seemed to have replaced the "this is the first day of the rest of your life" thoughts. I was already regretting going back to Sara's, and I was trying not to fixate on Beth too much (that evil bitch with her peach-colored nails). And I knew I was going to regret my visit to my parents, too—I knew that I'd want to leave the second I got there.

A woman came out for a smoke and gave me a little smile. She was in her mid-forties but attractive enough, in a New Age kind of way, with a blue scarf tied in her hair and some funky Native American-type earrings. I kind of wished that I smoked just then—we could share a cigarette, talk about the weather or how the ferry trip gave you time to think deep thoughts, and then maybe she'd invite me back to her ceramics studio or whatever. It would be great. But instead, I just smiled back. Hey, things weren't so bad! Jeez.

About ten minutes before the ferry pulled into Bremerton, I went and sat in the car. All of a sudden I was worried that the car wouldn't start, that I'd hold everyone back, so I started the engine early—I'm sure the guy behind me was thrilled by the cloud of blue smoke. I was first off the boat and up the hill. Go Celica go!

The Olympic Peninsula always seemed kind of bleak to me. A bunch of two-lane highways cutting through endless rows of trees with the occasional view of water. Maybe it just seemed like too much of a natural place to die, in a head-on with an old pickup truck, your last breath taken on the wet blacktop, rain and tears in your eyes, looking up at dark pine tree branches swaying in the wind.

My parents' house was located in one of these big new developments. The house had something like six bedrooms and eight bathrooms and my parents had no idea what to do with all the space. They had made such a big deal about me and my brother clearing all our stuff out of their old house in Tacoma and now they couldn't fill their new house. One bedroom had a Stairmaster, the other had a treadmill. No joke. Before, when I'd seen houses like this being built, I always wondered who would buy them. Well, now I knew.

My mom answered the door (big door, big entryway with a big brass chandelier). She gave me a hug and said, "Hi honey."

Phil came up behind her. When he saw the Celica, he said, "What the hell is that?"

"Uh, my car?"

I was just kind of standing there. Finally, they let me into the house.

We sat at the huge dining room table in the huge dining room—me at the head of the table with my parents on either side. They both looked healthy as hell. When I was in high school my mom had dyed her hair, but now she had let it go gray and it looked a lot better. And Phil looked younger than he had just a year before, when he was still putting in fifty-hour work weeks. He had obviously been working out. He was wearing a tight-fitting sweater that showed off his pecs. But then again, he'd always been pretty tough, pretty fit—he'd been in the Marines, served in Vietnam in the mid-60s, and I'm sure he could still bust out one hundred push-ups, no problem.

Anyway, by the heavy silence I could tell they knew something was up—they seemed to be waiting for an explanation. So I told them about the break up.

When I finished with my abridged version—appropriate for all audiences—my mom said, "Did she say why?"

"I don't know," I said. "Sort of."

"You two just grew apart."

"Yeah, I guess."

Phil was looking down at his lap and shaking his head. I think he'd always wanted a daughter, and Sara had seemed like a pretty darn good substitute.

"Oh dear," my mom said. "These things are hard."

I thought my mom was going to cry. Maybe they thought I was more upset than I actually was. Of course, I hadn't told them about the humiliating events of the last twenty-four hours. I hadn't told them about Darryl. I'm not sure they'd really understand the whole Darryl concept.

After a few minutes of silence, Phil sighed and stood up. "Want to see our new Gore-Tex jackets?"

I followed Phil into one of the first floor bedrooms, which had been transformed into the adventure travel room. Man, they had bought a lot of equipment—foldable walking sticks, high tech plastic boots, Gore-Tex jackets, thermal underwear, waterproof gloves, special sunglasses, brightly-colored backpacks, sub-zero sleeping bags—you name it, they had it.

Phil said, "I just hope my knee doesn't bother me too much."

"What about the Yeti?" I said.

"The what?"

"You know. Bigfoot. I heard he lives in Tibet."

"Oh," he laughed. "Right."

Phil wasn't really that bad a guy. Just kind of dense sometimes. I think that's what drove Nick crazy. No one had said anything about Nick yet. I wasn't sure if that was a good thing or a bad thing.

My mom walked into the room. "Is he showing you all his new stuff?"

"My new stuff?" Phil said. "You mean our new stuff." He sounded hurt.

My mom appealed to me. "I wanted to go to Italy. You don't need all this equipment for Italy."

Phil shook his head. "You've been to Italy. It's time to try something new for a change."

This is as close as they ever got to arguing. Even though I had been small, I could still remember the fights my mom had had with my dad—they'd been pretty animated. But my mom and Phil seemed fairly content—unless, of course, they were dealing with Nick.

At that point I told them that I was tired, that I needed to go to bed.

I went up into "my room." It was the room that Sara and I had shared a few times—it had a double bed. I closed the door. The doors in this house weighed about two ounces. You could put your fist through them if you wanted (Nick had done this once after a big argument with Phil). I sat down on the bed and looked at the whale prints my mom had put on the wall. They were new. I guess this was the whale room now.

Of course I already wanted to leave. But where else was I supposed to sleep? Fucking hell.

I went and brushed my teeth in the bathroom. The sink was supposed to look like a huge clam shell, and the faucet handles were like gold scallops or something. The fluorescent light was so bright against the white walls I felt like I was vibrating.

I got in bed and shut off the light. I started thinking about Kelly. I thought about Kelly naked. I felt better already. I should call Kelly and see how she was doing. And while I was at it, I should talk to Bob about his friend and the personal assistant job. I'd completely forgotten about that. It had sounded horrible when he had mentioned it, but how bad could it be? I knew I couldn't handle group living again. I also knew I wouldn't be able to get an apartment without a job—I'd tried that before and it didn't work. Yeah, live off some rich guy. Seemed like the best option I had at the moment. Yeah. Okay. I had a plan.

The next morning, I went out with Phil to look for an altimeter. We took his big new Ford F150 pickup. I had no idea why he needed a thirty-thousand-dollar truck with four-wheel drive and leather seats, a CD changer and six cup holders but whatever.

On the way over to the camping store, Phil finally mentioned Nick.

"You talked to your brother lately?"

"No," I said.

"We've been trying to reach him for the last week, but he hasn't called back. I talked to someone at his dormitory, so at least I know he's alive."

"I'm sure he's fine."

Phil shook his head. "I don't know what's wrong with that kid. Your mother is worried."

I didn't say anything. I knew that my mom was probably less worried than Phil. At least she was still able to communicate with Nick—I wouldn't be surprised if she had talked to him recently without Phil even knowing about it. Sometimes Nick would call and if Phil answered he'd hang up. You'd say, "Who was it?" And Phil would say, "I guess it was a wrong number." But I think he knew.

Poor Phil. He was totally clueless when it came to Nick. Once, after a shoplifting incident, Phil had invited one of his cop friends over to talk to Nick. Nick walked out. I think that had been a turning point between Nick and Phil—and Phil hadn't really known what to do since.

Phil sighed. "I just wish he could be a bit more considerate."

The camping store didn't have the exact model altimeter Phil wanted, so they had to special order it. I milled around and flipped through outdoors magazines while Phil talked to the salesperson. Then I ended up over near the hunting rifles.

They had quite a selection. Big guns, small guns. Guns with telescopes, guns with carved wooden handles. Guns with black barrels, guns with brown barrels. In other words, lots of guns.

I'd never even touched a gun. They scared me. A few times, when his parents were out, Dan would take one of his dad's shotguns out of the locked case (Dan knew where his dad hid the key). Dan liked to pump it and pull the trigger even though he knew this was bad for the mechanism. It made me jump every time. Dan would just laugh.

Phil said, "You in the market for a rifle, Keith?" Phil was a gun guy, too. He kept a .357 Magnum in the drawer of his bedside table.

"No," I said.

On the way back, Phil decided he should comment on my present situation.

"I got dumped by my girlfriend when I was your age."

I didn't know what to say. I said, "Oh yeah?"

Phil looked at me, then looked back at the road. "It took me a long time to recover from that. So be patient, and don't be too hard on yourself. I mean, in my case, it ended up being for the best. Otherwise, I wouldn't have met your mother!"

"Yeah," I said.

Phil smiled and nodded. I think we were both glad to have gotten that out of the way.

Later that afternoon, I called Kelly. When she came to the phone she said, "Where are you? We were all worried about you."

This made me feel a lot better. I explained that I had gone to my parents' house. Then I asked about Milo and she said he was okay, thanks for asking. When she asked me when I would be coming back, I explained my little plan to move in with Bob's friend. I thought she'd be more excited, but all she said was, "Oh."

"What?"

"Nothing. Do you want to talk to Bob?" She sounded cold and distant all of a sudden.

"Sure," I said. Before I knew it, she had put down the phone. What the fuck?

A moment later, Bob came on the line.

I said, "Hi, it's Keith, we met a few nights ago..."

"Right, right," Bob said. "What can I do for you?"

"Well, you mentioned that a friend of yours..."

"Oh, yeah, you're interested? Let me give you his number." Bob dropped the phone, then came back and gave me his friend's number. The guy's name was Chad.

"Chad's a real cool guy. Just explain that you know me."

"Got it," I said. "Thanks."

"Not a problem."

I hung up, slightly disturbed by Kelly's manner. But at least I had this Chad guy's number. I called it immediately and got his voicemail. I left a message.

That night my mom cooked a special meal—Shake 'N Bake. I'd been crazy about it when I was a kid, and she always cooked it for me on my birthday or after I'd been to the dentist or something. And we all knew Phil didn't really like it much, so it was extra special.

In the middle of dinner, the phone rang. My mom got it and then called out, "It's for you. Someone named Chad."

I picked up the phone. "Hello?"

"Hey Keith, this is Chad." The guy sounded kind of nasally, kind of hyper.

I said, "Oh, hey, thanks for calling back. Bob..."

"Yeah, just talked to him. So, cool. We should meet."

"Sounds good."

"Tomorrow?"

"Yeah, tomorrow works."

"Great." He gave me his address. "How 'bout around noon?"

"Sounds good."

When I hung up, my mom said, "Who was that?"

"Some guy who wants to give me a job."

"What kind of work?" Phil said.

"Um," I said. "I'm not sure yet. I'll find out more tomorrow."

"Seems awful late to be calling about a job," my mom said.

After dinner we all watched TV. First, we watched 60 *Minutes*. They were doing an expose on hazardous kid's toys (choking deaths, strangling deaths, fiery deaths) and Phil got really angry. So then we switched to some Jodie Foster movie where she was crawling around in the woods and mumbling in some kind of made-up language. My mom said, "Is she retarded?" and Phil said, "I read somewhere that she's a lesbian." And then I had one more night in the whale room, a big banana pancake breakfast, and the next thing I knew I was back on the ferry.

Taking the ferry back to Seattle was a whole different experience. As you get closer, the city slowly rises up in front of you, getting bigger and bigger. Sunlight was glinting off the tall skyscrapers. Yeah, I was coming back. Back to kick some ass.

Eight

Chad lived up on Queen Anne, one of the older neighbor-hoods in Seattle. Lots of big houses and tall trees and city and water views dropping away on all sides.

Chad's house was near the top of the hill, surrounded by a thick hedge. A brick driveway led up to a garage with ivy running up the side. Large plate glass windows faced the city skyline.

I climbed up the steps and rang the doorbell. A minute later, Chad appeared. He was on the cell phone. He smiled at me and nodded, then walked back into the house, leaving the door open. He was thin, in his early forties, going bald on top. He was wearing a turtleneck and loafers with little tassels.

I followed him through the dark wood entryway and into the living room, which was sparsely furnished with modern-looking furniture. Kind of Bauhaus or something. The blue-green lights of an expensive looking stereo glowed in the corner.

Finally, Chad was done with his phone call.

"Sorry about that," he said, closing the phone. ~ "Keith, right?"

"Right," I said.

He said, "Chad," and stuck out his hand.

We shook hands—he had a limp, sweaty handshake—and then he said, "Find the place okay?"

"Yeah, fine."

"Good, good." He seemed distracted, unsure how to proceed. "Um, so where should be start? This is the house..." He waved in the general direction of the kitchen, which I could see through a series of doors.

"Okay," I said.

"You want a tour?"

"Sure."

"It's kind of a mess. The cleaner comes tomorrow."

I started to follow him up a creaking wooden staircase, but then he stopped and turned around. "You don't need to see all that." He headed back down past me and turned toward the kitchen. I followed.

"This is the kitchen."

"Right," I said.

The kitchen was flooded with light. Lots of yellow tile and copper pots hanging from hooks. I felt like I was standing in the middle of one of Sara's home decorating magazines.

"The reason I want someone is that I'm pretty busy and otherwise stuff just doesn't happen."

"Uh huh."

"I had someone for a short while a few months ago but it didn't work out."

Chad reached into his pocket and removed a package of what at first looked like Life Savers. When he unwrapped the foil and held it out to me, I saw that they were Tums.

"Want one?"

"No thanks."

"Tropical fruit."

"What?"

"Tropical fruit flavor."

"Oh, right."

"They're a good source of calcium."

"Okay," I said.

He shrugged, took one for himself and popped it in his mouth.

Then, chewing on the tablet, he said, "Do you want to see where you'd be living?"

"Sure," I said.

"Great."

I followed him out the back kitchen door. We walked across a small courtyard, between rows of sickly-looking roses, to an adjoining portion of the house which looked like a recent addition.

"You have your own entrance. It's sort of a mother-in-law type deal. Completely private."

He opened the door, which was unlocked. I followed him inside.

He pulled back some heavy shades to reveal a large room with wall-to-wall carpet, a sofa and a dead potted plant. There was a walk-in closet and a bathroom and a small kitchenette. The place smelled musty.

He walked over to the couch and started pulling off the cushions. "This is one of those hide-a-bed things." He started yanking on the mattress but then put it back. "You get the idea."

It was as if he was a landlord or a realtor showing me the place—trying to sell me on it.

"So what would I be doing?" I said.

"Well you wouldn't have to cook or clean or do anything like that—I have people for that. I need someone who can run occasional errands, you know, dry cleaner, take the car in for an oil change, that sort of thing. Make sure there's some food around—you can just call and get it delivered. Be here for UPS and Fed Ex. I travel a lot, so I'd need you to be able to take me to the airport and pick me up. But I mostly just want someone around. Do you have a cell phone?"

"No," I said.

"Well, we'd have to get you one."

It bothered me that he had already made up his mind about all this—that he seemed to be assuming I'd take the job.

"And of course I'd pay you. Five hundred dollars a month, in addition to the free place to stay and whatever you want in terms of food. Bob said you don't have a job, right? So that would be perfect." His phone rang. He checked the number on the caller I.D. display and ignored it.

He continued: "I mean, I know I could go through an agency—that's what I did last time—but it ends up being too formal, and you don't know who you're going to end up with. I don't need a professional or anything. It's a pretty mellow job."

I nodded. I think he sensed that I was a bit uneasy. He said, "Well, I need to make a few calls. Feel free to wander around. Make yourself at home."

With that, he walked out.

I went into the kitchenette, ran water in the sink. After the pipes cleared—sputtering pops of air—I took a drink. The refrigerator was turned off and the door was closed, which I knew to be a bad idea. I opened the fridge door but immediately closed it again when I smelled the stench. I walked back into the main room.

I counted seven dead flies on the floor under the large plate glass window that faced into the courtyard. I wondered who had worked for Chad last, and why it "didn't work out."

I didn't really like Chad very much, but I guess it didn't matter. Something about the whole thing seemed a little creepy, though. I was trying to imagine myself going to the dry cleaners. But I couldn't really imagine getting another stupid cubicle job, either. I mean, what were my options? I could quit at any time. Ha.

I walked back into the house through the kitchen. I could hear Chad upstairs somewhere, talking on the phone. I went and sat on the black leather couch in the living room.

A while later, Chad walked in.

"Oh, here you are. Is that your car parked out front?"

"Yeah," I said.

"Awesome. I'm gonna have to borrow that sometime. I'd love to take that to valet parking." He laughed. "So what do you think?"

"Let's do it."

"Great. Great. Look, I gotta go out right now. Let me give you some keys." He walked out the of the room but kept talking. "You can just look around, move your stuff in, whatever."

"Okay."

He came back in and handed me a set of keys. "Take whatever you want from the fridge, too."

"Sounds good."

"Good, good. Well, it was nice meeting you. I've got a good feeling about this. I trust Bob." He smiled. "I'll see you tonight, okay?"

"Okay," I said.

"Okay, great."

As I listened to him pull out of the garage, I was hit by the crushing blow: had my life really come to this? Was I going to be someone's personal assistant?

I sat back into the couch and rubbed my eyes. Think temporary. This is just until I find something better. It beat living on someone's couch or moving back in with the parents. Or finding another stupid shit job. No, this was going to give me the space I needed. And some time to think.

I decided to take a full tour of the house. I opened every door, went into every room. There wasn't all that much to see, really. He had a cluttered office, a bedroom with clothes all over the floor, and all the other rooms looked untouched.

I checked out his closet. If I had known anything about clothing, I probably would have been impressed. But to me it was just a bunch of black suits.

There was a treadmill in one room, and a sauna built into the adjoining bathroom. In his office I found a photo of a good-looking blonde woman. The photo had been taken on the beach somewhere. The woman was shielding her eyes with one hand, squinting against the sun.

I glanced through some of his papers. I didn't even know what he did for a living and couldn't figure it out from any of the stuff in his office. He had one of those little golf putting kits. I played around with that for a while.

The stereo was pretty impressive. Too bad all his music sucked. Tom Petty and George Harrison. What a waste. I found an old Stones disc and cranked up "You Can't Always Get What You Want."

I went back to the kitchen and looked in the fridge. There was a half-empty bottle of Diet Coke and some moldy leftover Chinese food and that was it. I opened the cupboard and found some stale Fig Newtons. I ate those and then went out to the car.

I'd never even bothered to unload the Celica at my parents' house. It only took me a few trips to get all my stuff into my little mother-in-law apartment. The more I looked at it, the more I liked it. I realized that I'd never had a place all to myself. It was going to be cool.

I found some cleaning supplies under the kitchenette sink, and then spent a while scrubbing out my fridge. After that I was tired. I was still hungry but I was too lazy to go out for something. I fell asleep on the hide-a-bed.

I woke up at dusk. I could hear music and saw lights on in the house. I got up and brushed my teeth. Then I walked over.

Chad was in his office, flipping through some papers. He jumped when he saw me. "Shit. You scared me."

"Sorry."

"You get moved in okay?"

"Yeah."

"Great, great."

He had changed into a white dress shirt. Now that he wasn't wearing the turtleneck, I noticed that he had a long scar down his neck.

I said, "So what do you do?"

"Oh, lots of stuff," he said. He put his hands up and wiggled his fingers at me. "Got my fingers in lots of pies." Then he stood up. "Hey, I was thinking we could go out to dinner. My girlfriend Melissa wants to meet you. Did I mention Melissa?"

"No."

"You'll like her."

We took Chad's Explorer. The interior was littered with fast food wrappers and I had to push a bunch of newspapers and file folders off the passenger seat before I could even get in. When he backed out of the garage, a bottle of Pepto-Bismol slid out from under the seat and hit my feet. When I asked him what to do with it, he told me to put it in the glove compartment.

When I opened the glove compartment, there was an avalanche. The glove compartment was like a mini medicine cabinet: Imodium AD, Mylanta, Milk of Magnesia, Tylenol, Motrin, more Pepto, a large bottle of Tums. The guy must have had one fucked up stomach. I stuffed it all back in as best as I could.

Chad drove like a total idiot—hard on the gas and then hard on the brakes. I kept having to grab the dash. Between hard swerves and abrupt accelerations, I asked about Melissa and found out that she was a lawyer and that she lived on a houseboat. They had been dating "on and off" for about two years. But that was all I could get out of Chad—he seemed preoccupied.

Chad double-parked on a neighborhood street under the University Bridge and shut off the engine. He put on the flashers.

Chad said, "You want to come in?"

"Sure," I said.

Melissa was walking around barefoot on the shag carpet of the houseboat, talking on her cell phone. What is it with these people and their fucking cell phones?

I recognized her from the photo on Chad's desk. She was really good looking. Short dirty blonde hair held back by a pair of sunglasses (even though it was dark now). She was tall—as tall as Chad—and wearing a baggy UW sweatshirt and plastic soccer shorts. I also noticed a silver ankle bracelet, hanging loosely around her thin, shapely ankle. She'd maybe had a bit too much sun over the years but she still looked great.

She smiled at us but continued with the conversation for another minute or so. Then she got off. "Hi!" she said.

Chad said, "Hey," and gave her a kiss. Then he turned and said, "This is Keith."

"Hi," I said.

"Nice to meet you."

"I hope you know what you're getting yourself into," she said, and laughed.

"Don't scare him," Chad said.

"Be afraid," she said, bugging her eyes out at me. "Be very afraid."

We all just kind of laughed. Then she had to change. They disappeared into the bedroom.

I felt slightly unsteady—like I was lightheaded or something—but then I remembered: I was on a boat.

The place reeked of incense and perfumed candles—maybe to mask the smell of the marine septic system and creeping damp moldiness. The view was nuts, though. Water and city lights and the I-5 bridge towering overhead. I liked that. I liked looking out at the silvery water and at bridges and roads with lots of traffic. People rushing around while I just chilled back.

There was a rather large ski boat parked outside the houseboat. Beige and white with green stripes. It looked like something out of a Puff Daddy video. On the side it said, "Twinkle Toes."

I could hear them talking in the bedroom, a sort of low murmur. For some reason that made me think about Sara—made me remember the looks she would give me in private when people came over to visit. Quick, searching glances before she put her party face on and went out to talk to the crowd.

The mood had shifted by the time Melissa and Chad emerged from the bedroom. Melissa had changed into a slightly wrinkled blue dress that she kept trying to iron out with her hands. And all of a sudden, no one was talking.

This continued in the Explorer. I couldn't tell if they'd had an argument in the bedroom or what. All I knew was that I was glad to be sitting in the back seat. But I felt kind of like a little kid back there—a little kid whose parents weren't talking to each other. I fiddled around with the little chrome ashtray and ran the power window up and down.

The oppressive mood continued into the restaurant, which was some kind of new age California cuisine place. We all ordered but then Chad took way too long over the wine menu. I think I pissed him off by ordering a beer.

Chad sent the first bottle of wine back—power tripping on the poor waitress, who seemed bored and distracted—but appeared to be pleased with the next bottle that came to the table. We sipped at our drinks while we waited for the food, and Chad played with the bezel on his expensive-looking diver's watch. I wondered what that wine would do to his stomach. Then I got up and excused myself to go to the bathroom.

I aimed right in at that little pink deodorant thing. I liked doing that for some reason. Those things smelled kind of like candy. Candy and chemicals.

I washed my hands. Instead of paper towels, they had individual linen towels.

I was seriously thinking of walking out the back door at that point. Fuck these people. But I was buzzed and lightheaded and really hungry. What the hell. Go with the flow. I went back to the table.

Here's how the conversation went when I got back:

"I think Gary is screwing our new paralegal."

Chad, bored. "Yeah?"

"They used to be openly flirtatious. Now they just shoot each other knowing looks."

Chad was still playing with his watch. "Hmmm."

I was getting the feeling that Melissa annoyed Chad. Sometimes, Sara had annoyed me at times, too. But she didn't annoy me very much or even all that often, and I thought that was normal. But then she started acting like she was annoyed with me. From time to time, I'd catch her just staring at me with this blank expression on her face and I'd say, "What?" She would just shake her head and say, "Nothing."

I asked Melissa about the boat.

She smiled. "My dad gave it to me."

"That was nice of him," I said.

"I guess. Kind of a waste since I never use it."

"What's up with the name?"

"Twinkle Toes?" she laughed. "My dad used to call me that when I was a kid." She shook her head like she was remembering something. Then she said, "It's a nice boat. I'll take you out on it some time."

I couldn't tell if she was being fake nice or flirting or what. I sensed that Chad was making her uncomfortable—that she'd be different if he wasn't around.

Finally, our food came. I had ordered chicken something-

or-another and it was bony and had too much sauce and too many little onions that I couldn't stab with my fork—the inside would just shoot out.

No one said much while we ate. I ordered another beer and then went to the bathroom again. Then Chad took a long time scrutinizing the bill. Finally, he paid up and we got out of there.

After we dropped Melissa off, Chad reached into the glove compartment (skillfully containing the avalanche) and pulled out the bottle of Pepto Bismol. He unscrewed the top and took a big swig of the foamy pink liquid. He wiped his mouth with the back of his sleeve and said, "You single?"

I thought about Kelly, then said, "Basically."

"You're lucky," he said.

Nine

When we got back it was only about nine o'clock, so I called Kelly. I'd been thinking about her all the way back from the restaurant and I really wanted to see her.

I was glad when she answered—not Bob. So then I told her about moving in with Chad. She seemed kind of quiet, like something was bothering her. At first, I thought it had something to do with me, or maybe with me moving in with Chad. I remembered how abrupt she had been when I'd called from my parents' house. But then she whispered, "Milo got out."

"He got out?"

"He's gone. I can't find him." She sounded like she was going to cry.

"I'm sure you'll find him," I said.

"If he gets outside a dog could get him," she said. "And if they find out about him, they won't let me keep him."

"Want me to come over and help you look?"

"Could you?"

"Sure," I said.

"Oh thank you, thank you, thank you."

I drove over there. I had noticed that the Celica's clutch

was starting to slip a bit—I think it started after I tried to drag race that Camaro. Fuck. There was no way I was putting any money into this car. I'd drive it off a cliff first.

Kelly answered the door. She immediately put a finger up to her lips.

"Shh, they're watching a video. The kids are in bed."

She took my hand and led me upstairs. She was wearing baggy sweats and white tube socks. Her hair was wet from the shower and she smelled really good.

Her bedroom was just down the hall from the kids' room. Both bedroom doors were cracked open, so we had to be extra quiet.

Kelly had a small room with a single bed and a small desk. She had decorated the walls with tons of photos—some were of friends from back home, others were cut out of magazines. It reminded me of girls' lockers in high school.

She pointed to the closet door. "Look what he did."

The bottom of the door looked like it had been attacked by a rabid beaver. There were wood and paint chips on the carpet.

"Has he gotten out before?" I said.

She shook her head and bit her lip. She looked so good right then I had to really restrain myself. Maybe later if I could be the hero...

"So where have you looked?" I said.

"I've searched the whole upstairs. Well, everywhere except the kids' rooms."

"Should we look there first?"

"I don't know. I don't want to wake them."

"How long have they been in bed?"

She looked at her watch. "About an hour. Okay, but we have to be very very quiet."

Kelly pointed me in the direction of the older boy's room. His name was Kevin. She would search the younger girl's room.

I opened the door just enough so that I could squeeze through. The room was warm and I could hear the regular, heavy breathing of sleep.

Slowly, my eyes adjusted to the darkness. Kevin had a ton of toys. Big plastic toys. And they were all over the floor—it was like a minefield. Kevin had thrown off his covers and was curled into a fetal position in his Batman pajamas.

I got down on my hands and knees to look under the bed. Nothing as far as I could tell. So then, slowly, I made my way toward the closet, which was open.

I was almost there when I heard Kevin move. I froze. When I turned to look, it appeared that he was still asleep, though he had rolled over and was now facing in my general direction.

I waited several seconds, then started back toward the closet. I was starting to open the closet door when Kevin said, "Freeze."

I turned to see a pink and red and yellow Super Soaker leveled at me. Where the hell did that come from? He was sitting up in his bed now.

I put my hands up in the air. "Don't shoot."

"Who are you?"

"A friend of Kelly's."

I was impressed with his composure. At his age I think I would be screaming for my mom.

"What are you doing?" he said.

"Um," I said. "Looking for something?"

"What are you looking for?"

Luckily, that's when Kelly arrived on the scene. She switched on the light and said, "Kevin. Put the gun down."

Kevin wasn't taking orders from anyone. He said, "Why is he in my room?"

"Because he's helping me look for something."

"What?"

"Never mind what," she said.

She sat on the bed next to him and took the Super Soaker out of his hands.

"Come on," she said. He relented and lay back down. She put the covers back on him. Then she brushed his hair back and kissed him on the forehead. "Now go back to sleep," she said.

We were standing in the hallway, listening for movement in either of the kids' rooms.

"I hope Kevin goes back to sleep," Kelly said.

"Is he a problem?"

Kelly just rolled her eyes. Then she said, "Now what do we do?"

"Okay," I said. "We have to think like Milo. What does Milo like?"

"I don't know. Food. Any kind of food. Mostly raisins. He loves raisins."

"Have you tried looking in the kitchen?"

"No," she said, looking excited, like I was some kind of genius. "Let's go." She went running back down the stairs. I followed.

We opened all the kitchen cabinets, ran a broom handle under the refrigerator and looked behind the microwave. We went through all the drawers, looked behind the window shades and searched through the trash. No Milo.

Kelly slid down the side of the wall and slumped on the floor. She looked despondent.

I could hear explosions and yelling coming from the living room. Some stupid action movie blasting on a surround sound system with a huge subwoofer. But then I heard something else.

"Do you hear that?" I said.

"What?" she said. "I don't hear anything."

I listened some more. "Sounds like chewing to me."

I walked down the hall and discovered a large pantry. The chewing noises were very loud now.

"You didn't mention the pantry," I said.

Kelly came running up behind me. We started opening all the cupboard doors. A second later, Kelly squealed, "Milo!" She reached down and pulled him out of an instant oatmeal box he'd ripped to shreds.

She started rocking Milo back and forth in her arms. Milo was covered with oatmeal and brown sugar.

"Oh Milo, you really scared me, you really did."

Milo was licking his lips.

I heard the living room door slide open and then soundtrack music swelled into the hallway, followed by a burst of static and then silence. Then, before we could do anything, a woman appeared behind Kelly. I assumed it was Bob's wife.

"What's that?" she said, pointing a manicured finger at Milo. She looked half-scared, half-disgusted. She was wearing a lot of makeup and her hair was done up like the Bride of Frankenstein. Bob walked up behind his wife and put his hands on her shoulders.

"Hey Keith, how's it going?"

"Pretty good," I said.

"Did you meet Linda?" he said.

"No," I said. "Nice to meet you."

"Hi," she said, not taking her eyes off Milo.

"Chad said that you moved in already."

"Yup."

"What is that?" Bob said, suddenly noticing Milo. He wrinkled his nose. "Is that a rat?"

"He's a ferret," Kelly said. "Keith brought him over to show it to me."

"Uh, yeah," I said.

Linda said, "It's gross."

"He is not," Kelly said, intense hatred flashing across her face. "He's cute." With that, Kelly pushed Milo into my arms. Milo immediately started squirming around. I could barely hold onto him.

"He made quite a mess," Bob said, looking at all the open oatmeal boxes.

"Don't worry, I'll clean it up," Kelly said.

Just then, Kevin arrived on the scene with his Super Soaker, followed by his younger sister, who was wearing a pink bodysuit and green frog slippers.

Kevin pointed at me and said, "He was in my room." Then he noticed Milo and said, "What's that?"

"Don't touch it," Linda said. "It might have a disease."

Kelly started shoving me towards the front door.

"Thanks for coming over, Keith. I'll call you later."

She opened the front door and whispered, "It will just be for a little while, okay?"

Then she gave me a kiss, pushed me outside and closed the door.

Milo went nuts in the car. He started running around like a total maniac. I tried to grab him again, but he crawled into one of the big speaker holes in the door panels and disappeared. I didn't know what to do, so I fired up the car and started driving.

I heard all sorts of crazy chewing noises as I drove home. Then nothing. Then, all of a sudden, he was running up my pant leg. I almost ran into a parked car. I had to pull over.

I was trying to block his progress and get my pants off at the same time when the interior of my car was flooded with light. I turned to see that a cop car had pulled up behind me.

The cop got out, walked up and tapped my window with his flashlight.

I rolled down my window.

"Everything okay in there?"

I had just managed to get Milo out of my pants, which were now down at my ankles. I said, "I'm having a problem with my pet."

The cop looked at me and then looked at Milo. "Is that a rat?"

"No, it's a ferret."

"Huh," he said. Then he said, "Have you been drinking?"

"No sir."

"I'm glad to hear that. License and registration, please."

I suddenly worried about the car—it occurred to me that it could be stolen. I explained that I had just bought the car and gave him what I had—all with one hand. With the other hand, I pinned Milo to my lap.

He looked it over and handed it all back.

"Drive safely," he said. "And get that thing on a leash."

The lights were still on when I got back to Chad's house. I didn't want to go through the house with Milo, so I walked around the side.

I spent my first night in my new place with that crazy rodent running all over the place. I drifted off to sleep to awful scraping and chewing noises. I didn't think Milo could escape, but I didn't particularly care, either. At one point I woke up to heavy breathing in my ear—he had stuck his nose into my ear like he was trying to burrow into my head or something. I grabbed him and got him into something like a headlock, and after a while he seemed to settle down. Then we both fell asleep.

Ten

I woke up to see Chad standing over me.

"Sorry. I knocked but you didn't answer."

I sat up. There was a sick, sweet smell. It took me a second to realize that it was Chad's cologne.

"I got you a phone." He dropped a cell phone in my lap. "The number is written on the back."

I rubbed my eyes. "What time is it?" I said.

"Eight thirty. Hey, I got an errand for you. We need a new water filter for the icemaker in the fridge. They got 'em at Home Depot. Here's the part number."

He handed me a scrap of paper. I could barely read his writing.

"Alright, champ. I'm heading to work. I'll catch up with you later."

I just sat there for a while. I looked at the cell phone. I'd never had one before. This one looked very Star Trek, with the little flip-up face plate. I turned it over. There was a Post-it note on the back with the number written on it.

I heard a scratching/rustling noise, and then Milo climbed out of the couch. He'd chewed a hole in the arm and ripped out a bunch of the stuffing—he'd made himself a little burrow in there.

He looked up at me for a second and then started gnawing on my finger.

"You're hungry, huh?" I was starting to get used to the way he smelled—he smelled a lot better than Chad, that's for sure. And he was kind of cute.

I went into the house and got those stale Fig Newtons. Then I came back and shared them with Milo.

I thought about calling people to tell them my new number, but it was too early. I ended up falling back asleep.

When I woke up again my cell phone was ringing. It was Chad.

"Hey Keith buddy, can you check on something for me?"

"Sure," I said. "What?"

"There's a Rolodex in my office. I need the number for Dick Dawson. Call me back." He hung up.

I went into the house, found Dick's number in the Rolodex and wrote it down. Then I went back to my place.

Ten minutes later, my cell phone rang.

"What's the problem? Couldn't find the number?"

"No," I said. "I don't have your cell phone number."

"Oh, right." He gave me his number. Then I gave him the number he wanted.

"So how's everything going? Get that water filter yet?"

"Not yet," I said. I was trying not to get pissed off.

"Alright, well, gotta go." He hung up.

I checked my watch. It was almost noon. Shit. Milo

wasn't around. I reached into the hole in the couch. I could feel his little warm body in there, sleeping.

I drove down to Home Depot on Aurora Avenue, which is basically a long, shitty strip. Lots of stoplights. The clutch was really starting to vibrate badly as I pulled away from stop lights.

When I walked into Home Depot, I got lost immediately, wandering around the long aisles of towering crap with my little scrap of paper. Finally, some guy in an orange apron led me over to the right aisle. It turned out that they didn't have the right filter—the guy said it had been discontinued or something. But he had one that would work—that "should work," anyway. Twenty bucks, though. Chad and I hadn't worked out the money stuff yet, which kind of sucked. And I was starting to run out of money, fast. What else was I going to do? I paid up and got out of there.

I decided to drop by Big Bob's Tires to see Dan. I also wanted to talk to Carl about the clutch.

Dan smiled when he saw me pull up. He walked over as I got out of the car. He had a big grease smear on his forehead.

"Nice car," he said. "What's up?"

"Nothing."

"Tammy told me you were alive. What've you been up to?"

I explained the whole thing about Chad.

"So what, you're a personal assistant or something?"

"Not really," I said. "It's more mellow than that."

Dan started laughing. "Man, I'm gonna have to start calling you Kato."

"What?"

"You know, Kato Kaelin. The O.J. guy?"

"Fuck you," I said.

Dan couldn't stop laughing. "Does the dude drive a white Bronco?"

I could feel my face getting red. "An Explorer, actually."

This was too much for Dan. He almost fell over laughing. When he calmed down a bit, he said, "Watch out. Next thing you know, he's gonna need you to be his alibi."

"Yeah, yeah," I said.

"Seriously, man. That's kind of weird, you know."

I couldn't help it, I was getting angry. "Well what the fuck else was I supposed to do?"

"I'm sorry, man." Dan was just shaking his head and laughing. "I'm just giving you shit." Then he nodded at the Celica. "How's this thing holding up?"

"Clutch is slipping."

"Yeah? I think Carl put it in himself. Maybe he didn't adjust it right."

"Is he here?"

"Naw. He's at lunch. I'll tell him when he gets back, though. I'm sure he can fix it for you."

"That would be cool," I said.

Dan laughed.

"What?"

Dan shook his head. "Kato."

"Man, fuck you."

"I'm sorry." Then he said, "Hey, I should get back to work."

"Here, let me give you my number." I pulled out my cell phone, which still had the number written on the back.

"You got a cell phone now? You're killing me, man." He just shook his head as he wrote down the number.

I drove away. Dan had pissed me off with that Kato stuff—though I admit it was kind of funny. I had a feeling that was going to stick.

On the way back to Chad's I went to Safeway and bought myself some food—frozen pizza, frozen burritos, Corn Flakes and milk and bananas. They didn't have any ferret food in the pet section, so I got Milo some dried cat food.

When I got back to the house, there was a VW bus parked out front. Painted on the side were the words: TERRAPIN CLEANING SERVICES.

Inside, some guy was mopping the floor. Kind of a hippie, with flip-flops and long, matted hair sticking out the sides of a Rastafarian hat.

"Hi," I said.

The guy stopped mopping. "Hello."

"I'm Keith."

"Josh."

"You the cleaning guy?"

He smiled. "I'm the cleaning guy."

"I'm..." And then I didn't know what to say.

"Yeah, Chad told me."

"Oh," I said. "Right."

The guy was just standing there, smiling and holding the mop over the bucket, the water was going drip, drip, drip. I wondered how much acid he had done over the years.

"Well, good to meet you," I said.

"You too," he said.

Milo ate the cat food hungrily. After that, he ran around in circles for about twenty minutes and then disappeared back into the couch.

I decided I should call everyone and give them my new number. My mom sounded happy to hear from me—though she seemed a little concerned about my living situation and my lack of any real income. I was going to have to figure out a better way to explain it to people. Sara wasn't there so I left a message. Kelly wasn't home either. I didn't know who else to call. Depressing.

And then, for the first time in a long time, I realized that I had nothing to do. No work, no Sara-related social engagements, no errands. Boredom. I liked it. I lay back on the hide-a-bed and stared at the cracks in the ceiling.

Sometime later my cell phone rang. I was expecting it to be Chad again, but when I picked it up, the earpiece exploded with the sound of a loud, long belch. And even though I hadn't heard from him in weeks, I knew right away that it was my brother. Nick.

"Dude, wassup?" Nick was laughing, proud of himself. "Whew," he said. "Sorry about that."

"Hi Nick," I said.

"Hey," he said. I heard a girl's voice in the background, and laughter. Nick covered the phone to say something and then came back and said, "Yo. So what's up?"

"Not much," I said. "What's up with you?"

"Nothing, man. Just wanted to check in with my big bro."

"Cool," I said.

"Yeah, man. I tried your old number last night, but Sara got all weird on me, said I should talk to you. So then she gave me Dan's number, but when I talked to those guys, they said you weren't living there anymore. I finally got your number from mom, who said you were like a personal assistant or some shit like that?"

"Kind of," I said.

"Kind of?" he said. "So what happened with Sara? Mom said you were having problems or something."

"We're not having problems," I said. "We broke up."

"Serious?"

"Serious."

"Damn," Nick said. "So what, she kicked you out?"

"Not exactly," I said.

"What then?"

"I don't know," I said. "I moved out."

"Yeah? Well you know what I always say."

"No. But I can guess."

He started an enthusiastic rendition of Dr. Dre's *Bitches Ain't Shit*.

"Please stop," I said.

I heard some more laughter in the background. Nick covered the phone again and then came back on. "So what's up with this personal assistant shit?"

"I don't know," I said. "I needed a place to live."

"Yeah, but isn't that kind of gay?"

"Um..."

"Sorry, dude. I just can't picture it. Anyway, I'm coming up to Seattle. Either tomorrow or the next day. See Tony, hang out with you, get my bike, that kind of thing. That cool?"

"Yeah," I said. "Sounds cool."

"Right on," he said, and there was more laughter in the background, along with some yelling. "Hey man, I gotta go. But I'll call back later. Let you know when I'm gonna show up."

"Sounds good," I said.

"Alright, man. Later." And then he hung up.

Nick. With everything else, I'd almost forgotten that he was coming. And I'd almost forgotten about the bike. I knew I should have said something about it, but I hadn't figured out how to break it to him just yet. Well, I'd think of something. Then again, maybe I wouldn't.

Chad got home a while later—I saw the lights go on, heard him put on some Dire Straits or some crap like that. I waited a bit and then I went over with the water filter.

Chad seemed distracted. He was looking over some papers in his study and chewing on some more Tums. He was wearing these goofy reading glasses that made him look like a total dork.

I held up the water filter.

"Great," he said. "Just put it in when you get the chance."

"Put it in?"

"Yeah."

"Oh, okay."

"What?" he said, looking up.

"Nothing," I said.

He went back to whatever he was reading.

"By the way, it was twenty dollars."

He waved his hand. "Just keep your receipts. We can even up later."

I didn't know what to say. So, angry and humiliated, I walked out.

The cell phone was making me popular. Dan called with Carl's address, saying that he was expecting me to drop by to check out the Celica. And later on, Kelly called. She wanted to come visit Milo. She was nervous about trying to take him back. She thought they were on to her, that they were suspicious. She couldn't talk. She wanted me to come pick her up.

I explained that I needed to take the car to Carl's house first. She sighed and told me to hurry.

I heated up a frozen burrito in the microwave and then drove over to Carl's house. He lived up in Greenwood—no sidewalks, cars parked on the lawn.

I parked and walked up the front walk. The door was open—just the screen was closed. I was about to push the doorbell when a little kid walked up to the screen door. He was wearing a hockey helmet and ski goggles.

"Hi," I said. "Is your dad here?"

The kid just stared at me. I didn't know what to do. I rang the doorbell.

Carl showed up with a can of Rainier in his hand. "Hey. Keith, right?"

"Yeah," I said.

He started nudging the kid out of the way with his leg. "Out of the way, Ben. Let the man in."

The kid backed away from the door. Carl opened the screen door for me and I walked in.

"Yeah, so Dan tells me the clutch is slipping."

"Yup," I said. "Vibrates pretty bad when you pull away from a stop."

"But otherwise, the car's cool?"

"Yeah."

"Cool. Well, let me put my shoes on and we'll take a look. Wanna beer?"

"Sure," I said.

Carl jacked up the front of the Celica and slid under with a shop light and some wrenches.

"Yeah," he said. "Shit, sorry about that."

"Don't worry about it," I said.

I was sitting in a lawn chair, sipping my Rainier. It was a nice night out. A light breeze brought the smell of freshly cut grass.

A few minutes later, a Nissan pickup pulled in next to the Celica and a woman got out with a bag of groceries. She was maybe four feet ten and had a bad haircut, but she was kind of cute. She said hi to me and then kicked one of Carl's feet.

"Hey!" Carl yelled from under the car.

"What are you doing?" she said.

"What does it look like?"

She just smiled at me and shook her head. Then she walked into the house.

I thought to myself: this is domestic bliss. The American dream and all that bullshit. I tried to imagine Sara and I living like this, but I couldn't. Didn't seem too bad, though.

Carl slid back out a few minutes later.

"That should do it," he said.

"Great."

"Hey, want a bong hit? A friend hooked me up with some killer new weed from Oregon."

"Sounds good to me," I said.

I don't know if it was the pot or what, but after that, the clutch felt really good. Like solid, man. I was one with the clutch plate mechanism.

When I showed up at Kelly's, she said, "Your eyes are glowing."

I said, "Oh shit," and put my hand over my mouth to giggle like I was a little girl. It was a joke—the hand over the mouth. A joke only I would get.

Then I said, "Is it cool if I use the bathroom?"

"No," she said. "Let's go."

We didn't talk much in the car. The pot was wearing off and I felt tired. I kept yawning—really big embarrassing yawns—the kind of yawns where your mouth is wide open and you're trying to get it to hurry up and close again.

Chad was coming out the front door when we pulled up.

I was Mr. Congeniality. "Hey Chad," I said. "This is..."

Chad said, "We've met."

Kelly didn't say anything. She looked down at her feet.

I probably should've known everything then, but my brain doesn't work that way. Heavy denial mode always kicks in—I think this is what allowed me to live with Sara for two years. But common sense took over once we got into my little mother-in-law.

When I asked her about it, Kelly just shrugged. "We had a thing." She was snuggling with Milo.

"A thing?" I said. "What's a thing?"

"I don't know how you say it," she said. "A fling?"

"But then," I said. "How come..." I didn't know what to say. I felt like I'd been punched in the head. Finally, I said, "So what, did Bob set you guys up or something?"

"Bob doesn't know. They were on vacation."

"Vacation," I said.

"Yes. They went to Hawaii. Tammy and I were supposed to go on a road trip, but then Tammy couldn't."

"So you hooked up with Chad instead?"

"Hooked?" she said. "What is hooked?"

I said, "What about Melissa?"

Kelly shrugged. "They'd split up. That's what Chad told me, anyway. I don't know."

"Okay," I said.

"Can we not talk about it? He's an asshole and I don't want to think about it. It's bad enough that you live here."

Can things not be messy if you don't want them to be messy? Can you just ignore something if you want? And if you ignore it, will it go away? Will it not even exist?

I don't know what we did then. Nothing, I guess. All this talk about Chad seemed to knock the energy out of both of us.

And so now there was this thing between us. It was like we were underwater, like we were deep sea divers in full scuba gear, looking at each other through little scuba masks.

We still ended up having sex, but it was the kind of tired, unenthusiastic sex that you have when you've been with someone for a long time—like the of sex I'd been having with Sara for the last year or so. Except it was weird, tired sex. I kept thinking about Chad. How fucked up is that? And then I'd find myself thinking about Sara. And then I'd try to focus back on Kelly but that just made me start thinking about Chad again.

Later, Kelly woke me up.

"You have to drive me home."

So then we were back in the Celica. Dark empty roads, slick with fresh rain. I felt fine as long as the lights were green, as long as I could roll through four-way stops, but all the red lights made me uncomfortable, made the silence between as all that more obvious.

When I kissed Kelly goodnight, we both had our eyes open, and I realized that it was going to take some effort on my part to get past all this stuff—effort I wasn't sure I wanted to make. I had the feeling Kelly was thinking the same thing. She didn't look back at me before she went in the door.

Driving back to Chad's, I felt strangely happy. It didn't seem like the right thing to be feeling, but that's what I felt. Happy. Goofy, giddy happy. I started whistling. Then, on an empty two-lane road, I took a corner too fast, hit the brakes too late, and went into a spin.

Somehow, I didn't hit anything. I came to a stop on the shoulder with the engine stalled out and all the idiot lights glaring red. I shut off the ignition and just sat there—my heart pounding, my skin covered with a layer of cool sweat.

And then I started laughing. It took me a while to stop.

Eleven

Sara called me the next morning. She was happy that I had found a place to stay and wanted to "do lunch." I agreed to meet her at a bagel place over by Green Lake that afternoon.

I decided I had better try to install that water filter on the refrigerator. I fed Milo and then crossed the court-yard and entered the kitchen.

I had no idea where the filter even went. It was a huge refrigerator and I almost killed myself trying to pull it away from the wall—and I scratched up the hardwood floor pretty bad in the process.

When I finally located the filter, I saw that, of course, the one I had purchased was completely different. Fuck.

Chad walked in, whistling. He was wearing a silk kimono.

"Keith buddy," he said.

"Hi Chad."

He opened the fridge—ignoring its somewhat skewed placement—and looked inside. "We've got to get some food in this place."

I thought about the food I had bought for myself but said nothing.

He closed the fridge and then looked at my filter. "That's not the right one."

I didn't feel like explaining, didn't feel like defending myself. I said, "They said this would work."

"Hmmmm. Let's see."

Chad yanked off the old filter. Water started shooting everywhere. He was trying to get it back on and yelling, "Didn't you shut off the water?"

"What?" I said. "No."

"Shit." He dropped the filter and ran out of the room. I tried to stop the water with my thumb but it didn't work—the water just rushed down my arm and continued to fall on the floor. I felt like I was in an old Brady Bunch episode or something.

The water went off a minute later and Chad returned. The front of his robe was all wet. I was soaked, too. At least he seemed to think it was funny.

"You gotta turn the water off first," he said.

"I'll remember that next time."

He said, "Yeah, remember that." And then he punched me in the shoulder.

I watched as Chad forced on the new filter. It wasn't pretty, but it seemed to hold.

"There we go," he said. "I'll go turn the water back on. Yell if there's a problem."

"Okay," I said.

He disappeared. A minute later he walked back into the room.

"No problems?"

"Seems okay to me."

"Good," he said. "Well, that was fun."

I was glad to see that he was in a good mood. But it

almost seemed like he was taking a good cop/bad cop approach to me. Maybe he was just moody. Or maybe he was manic depressive—maybe he was medicated.

Anyway, I didn't really like the idea of being his friend, but I didn't want to be totally confrontational all the time, either. I was hoping to find some kind of middle ground. I'd heard that people who were kidnapped often begin to love their captors—I think there's even a word for it. Also, I'd been thinking about *The Great Gatsby* lately—I was starting to feel like he was Gatsby and I was Nick Carraway, and I didn't like that idea much. And then there was the whole thing with him and Kelly. I didn't even want to think about that.

Since he was wearing the kimono, I got a better look at his scar. It went down pretty far. I said, "So what's happened to your neck?"

"Oh this?" he said, pointing to the scar, as if I could have been referring to something else. "Motorcycle accident. Used to race Ducatis." To illustrate this, Chad started making revving motions with his wrist, grimacing and getting into a racing tuck. "Yeah, slid out in a corner and went down hard."

"Ouch," I said.

"Yeah," Chad said. "The thing about motorcycle helmets is, they protect your head but they also bounce—if you slide out, your head turns into a basketball. Anyway, I almost died. I was in the hospital for three months."

"That sucks."

"Actually, it was a life changing experience for me. That's when I decided to do something with my life, make something of myself. If it hadn't been for that accident, who knows where I'd be now."

It was hard for me to not roll my eyes at this, but I managed. I said, "That's cool."

He looked down at his wet kimono. "Well, I'm gonna go get changed."

"Alright," I said.

"Oh yeah, listen. I need you to pick up something for me. I'm not going to have time." Chad went over to the counter and wrote out an address for some place down in Georgetown. He handed it to me and said, "You want to speak to Joey."

"Joey," I said. "Got it."

After he walked out, I looked down at the floor, which was sopping wet. I guess that was my responsibility. I went to look for a mop.

I drove down to Georgetown—past the big red cranes in the harbor that look like spaceships invading from outer space, past the giant steam plant and factories and sprawling chain outlet stores.

The address Chad had given me was in a big warehouse area. I parked next to a loading dock, got out and walked up to a battered steel door. I rang the buzzer and looked up at the security camera.

After a minute or so, a big guy with a beard appeared at the loading dock.

"Keith?" the guy said.

"Yeah."

"Okay. Hold on a second."

The guy disappeared, then came and opened the door. He was wearing a plaid shirt, jeans and a big Harley Davidson belt buckle.

He handed me a heavy manila envelope. It was taped shut.

"Here ya go."

"Thanks," I said. "So I guess you're Joey."

"That's me." Then he nodded at my Celica. "That your car?"

"Yeah," I said.

"I used to have one of those. That an eighty-two?"

"I think."

"Same as mine. Same color and everything." He walked over to the Celica. "What happened to the seat?"

"It was like that when I got it."

He nodded, then took out a pack of cigarettes. He offered me one but I said no thanks. Then he pulled out a Zippo lighter. He lit his cigarette with a slight flourish and put the lighter on the hood of my car. What was that all about?

He blew out some smoke and said, "We've been having a bunch of kids dealing drugs out here."

"Oh yeah?"

He nodded and took another pull on his cigarette. Then he turned back to consider my car again.

"I totaled mine." He shook his head. "I was fucking shitfaced."

And then he seemed to become aware of something behind me. I turned to see a brand-new BMW approaching. It drove right up to us. I jumped about a foot when the car honked.

There was a lot of glare coming off the windshield, but I was able to make out the shape of a smallish woman behind the wheel. She looked like a model or something—lots of makeup, and her hair was all poofy. She appeared to be laughing.

Joey was just smiling and shaking his head. He started toward the car, but then the woman shifted into reverse and started backing away. Joey walked after the car, then sprinted forward and caught it—putting his hands on the hood. The woman stopped and rolled down her window and they exchanged a few words. Then she rolled the window back up, swung the car around and sped off.

Joey walked back to me just shaking his head. At that point a phone started ringing inside the warehouse. He said, "Oh shit." He pulled out a long keychain and started looking through his keys. Finally he found the right key, got the door open and ran inside.

I looked down at his Zippo, which was still on the hood of my car. I picked it up and took a closer look.

AS I WALK THROUGH THE VALLEY OF THE SHADOW OF DEATH I WILL FEAR NO EVIL FOR I AM THE EVILEST SON OF A BITCH IN THE VALLEY.

On the other side it said: U.S. MARINE CORPS

I waited for a while, then went and rang the buzzer. Nothing. I waited some more and then gave up. I put the Zippo on the loading dock and got out of there.

I told this story to Sara at lunch.

"Sounds really weird," she said.

I shrugged.

"What was in the envelope?"

"I don't know," I said. "I didn't open it."

"You didn't?" She seemed surprised.

"No," I said.

"I would have."

"Really?"

She nodded. "Definitely."

"I'd rather not know," I said. And it was true. I'd put the envelope on Chad's desk.

Sara shook her head. "Sounds like you have a very strange arrangement with this Chad person."

We were sitting on a bench outside, watching the roller bladers and strollers circle around Green Lake.

Sara was wearing her usual Saturday outfit—jeans, a sweatshirt and a Mariners baseball cap. She always pretended she was a big Mariners fan—I have no idea why. She never went to or watched any of the games.

Sara had been living near Green Lake when we first met. In fact, this bench had been the site of one of our first dates—and one of our first arguments. Sara had been convinced that we had actually met once before. I hadn't known what to say to that—I mean, I knew it wouldn't come off too well if I admitted to not remembering her. But I didn't, and I said as much. She had been hurt. So then I tried to pretend that I did, in fact, remember meeting her. But I couldn't produce any details about this meeting, and that only made things worse. Sometimes I got the feeling that I had never really recovered from this incident—that she would always hold it against me.

So we'd done the awkward silence thing on this bench before. It almost seemed natural. But as we sat there, eating the bagels and not talking, I started to get the feeling that some kind of announcement was coming. I knew Sara—knew how she operated. When she turned to look at me again, I thought: here we go...

"I'm sorry about the other day. I would have let you stay but..." She hesitated.

"Beth doesn't like me," I said.

"Well, that's part of it." She bit her lip.

I could tell that wasn't what she had been meaning to say. And suddenly, I didn't want to know. It was like Chad's envelope. Some things are better left unopened, unexamined.

Sara said, "The reason..." and then trailed off. I just waited.

"Well, I don't know how else to say this except Beth and I are, well, we're in love."

"We're..." I said. And then it hit me. Duh. I'd known that Beth was bisexual. I just hadn't really thought about it. Well, now I felt like an idiot.

"Are you okay?" Sara said.

"Yeah," I said. "Why?"

"You don't look okay."

"Oh," I said. "Sorry."

I had some questions but I sure as hell wasn't going to ask them. They'd just make me look and feel like more of an idiot.

"It started a while ago, and at first I thought..."

"That's okay," I said. "You don't have to explain anything to me."

"You're angry."

"I'm not angry."

"Yes you are. I know you."

"I'm not."

"Don't be angry."

"Well, I'm gonna get angry if you keep telling me not to be angry."

After that we just sat there. A seagull came and picked at a cheeseburger someone had thrown onto the ground. Pickle, catsup, mustard, cheese, beef, bun—it was all there. The seagull seemed mostly interested in the bun—maybe he'd heard about the whole mad cow disease thing. Another seagull came and they started playing tug of war with the bun.

"I should go," I said.

"You sure you're not angry?"

"No," I said. "I mean, yes."

And then I got up and walked away.

For the rest of the day, I felt like I'd had a lobotomy. I had trouble thinking. I walked around in circles. I stared at things.

Milo provided a bit of distraction. Milo was a cool dude.

"Hey Milo," I said. "Chicks suck. Remember that."

Let's see now—I'd been dumped for a woman, and my boss/landlord had been sleeping with my present girlfriend before me. Nice! It was convenient, really—if I started to fixate too much on one embarrassment, I could just think about the other humiliation for a while.

After Milo fell asleep, I walked outside and wandered around the backyard. Chad wasn't home. That was lucky.

If he'd come up and asked me to do something for him I probably would have punched him.

I was staring at a bush when the guy who lived next door walked up to the fence. It wasn't a very high fence—maybe five feet. So we could see each other eye to eye.

"You a friend of Chad's?" he said.

"Well, kind of," I said. "I'm living here."

"Oh," the guy said, nodding like he understood everything. He was an older guy—probably in his seventies. He had blotches all over his face. "I'm Ed, by the way."

"Keith," I said. I wanted to say, "Fuck off, Ed, you're bugging me," but I didn't.

"Nice day," he said.

"Yeah."

"Chad's something, isn't he?"

"He is," I said.

"A shame about his father."

His father? Huh? I said, "I guess I don't know what you're talking about."

"His father died two years ago. Cancer. Left him the house. His business. Everything."

"Oh," I said.

Ed frowned. "A friend of mine told me that Chad had already squandered most of his father's money on stupid schemes. I wouldn't be surprised if the bank already owns the house."

"Huh," I said.

"I mean, what does Chad know about business? He's been a freeloader all his life."

I shrugged.

Ed shook his head. "His father was a great man. We used to play golf."

"Cool," I said. "Golf."

A fly started buzzing around Ed's face. Ed made a few pathetic attempts to swat it away. When the fly finally went away, he seemed to have lost his train of thought. He said, "Anyway, nice talking to you."

"Yeah," I said.

The old guy waddled back into his house.

Okay. Information overload. I needed to take a nap. I went in and lay down on the hide-a-bed.

I ate frozen pizza for dinner. I didn't have a TV, so I started reading some of my old Kurt Vonnegut books that I found in one of my boxes. These went back to high school—I had all of Vonnegut's books. In fact, Vonnegut was the reason I became an English major when I got to college. The only problem was I never found any other writers I liked as much as Vonnegut.

I made it all the way through *Cat's Cradle* and was starting in on *Breakfast of Champions* when Chad called. It was a bit past midnight.

Chad was drunk at some bar. He and Melissa had gotten in a fight and he wanted me to come pick him up. I asked him why he didn't just take a cab, but he said, "No money." I thought about what Ed had said and then I told him I'd get down there as soon as I could.

The club was this big cheesy place down near Lake Union. I had to get past a bouncer in a tuxedo at the reception desk and then walked through a dining area with red candles on all the tables. I found him sitting at the bar with some skinny, Filipino-looking girl with a pimply forehead.

"Keith, Keith, Keith," he said, putting his hand on my shoulder. Then he said, "This is Tanya."

Tanya and I said hi.

"Keith is my chauffeur," he said, laughing.

Ha ha. No one said anything. Chad got up and excused himself to go to the bathroom. He literally staggered out of the room.

Tanya and I just stood there, smiling vaguely at each other. Finally, she said, "You work for Chad?"

"I guess," I said.

"He's funny."

"Yeah," I said.

I looked out at the water. A row of sailboats, bobbing gently up and down in the water. Two people were dancing out on the deck. I guess they were piping music out there. How romantic.

When Chad came back, he said, "So, are we going?"

I couldn't tell if the question was directed at me or Tanya. Tanya and I both shrugged.

"We're going, then," Chad said. And then Chad asked me if I could pay the tab.

"Sure," I said. "No problem."

He'd run up over a hundred dollars' worth of drinks. I put it on my credit card and asked for a receipt.

When we got out to the Celica, Chad said, "What a

total piece of shit. I love it." He had his arm around Tanya. "Don't you love it?" he said to Tanya. "Isn't it great?"

Tanya nodded but she looked more confused than amused. We got in—the two of them climbing in back.

"Home, James," Chad said.

We were half-way to Chad's house when there was a disagreement in the back of the car about where we were actually going. After a moment, Chad said, "Hey Keith, head for West Seattle, would ya?"

I swung a fast, hard U-turn, which made the tires squeal.

Chad said, "Easy, buddy." I just glared at him in the rear-view mirror.

We ended up way out in West Seattle, parked in front of a bleak two-story apartment building. Chad and Tanya got out of the car. Chad said, "Can you hold on a minute?"

They walked up the steps to one of the apartments, and then stood on the landing for a long time. The girl had her hand on the doorknob. Then she opened the door and they went inside. Fuck. I shut off the engine.

The street was totally quiet. After a while, a kid came by on skateboard, his wheels going ca-clack, ca-clack, ca-clack on the sidewalk.

I couldn't fucking believe this. I mean, it was almost funny. Funny but not funny.

I started thinking about what Ed had told me. And I started thinking more about the whole Gatsby thing. The parallels were definitely there. But who was Daisy? What was the green light?

One thing that always bothered me about *The Great Gatsby* was that Nick Carraway was basically Gatsby's pimp. That never seemed to bother Carraway. Well, it bothered me.

I was about to fire up the Celica and drive away when Chad came back out of the apartment. He came back down the stairs and got in the car.

"Sorry about that," he said.

A few blocks later, I had to pull over so he could puke. When he got back in the car, he just slumped on the floor where the front passenger seat had been. He burped and then pulled out his handy little roll of Tums.

We drove for a while and then I said, "I talked to Ed today."

"Who?"

"Ed. Your neighbor."

He waved his hand in the air. "Ed? Ed's an idiot. Don't listen to Ed."

"He mentioned something about your father."

"My father's dead."

Chad didn't seem to want to say any more after that, and I didn't feel like asking any more questions—didn't feel like bringing up the whole thing about him being a freeloader and a liar.

As we came out of the Aurora tunnel, that huge Pepsi sign rose up in front of us like a big red, white and blue sun. Like Colonel Klink's monocle on the 4th of July. Like a one-eyed Doctor T. J. Eckleburg, staring at me.

Twelve

The next day I got a call from Sam at my old job. He'd been trying to track me down for a few days and finally got my new number from Sara. After I explained about me and Sara, Sam told me why he'd called—he and Cathleen were having a housewarming party that night and wanted to invite me. I hadn't heard that they'd moved in together, so I congratulated him on that. I knew it would be one of those dull work crowd parties (and it seemed kind of weird, this being a Sunday night) but I told him I'd try to make it. I thought maybe I'd bring Kelly if she was up for it.

So far that morning there had been no signs of life from Chad. That fuck. I kept a low profile—I stayed in the mother-in-law and played with Milo. But after a while I was bored and antsy. I decided to get out of the house for a while.

It sucked, though. I didn't have that many places I could go. I couldn't go to Sara's place, and I couldn't go over to Dan's place because of the whole thing with Darryl. On Sundays Sara and I used to go out to Discovery Park and walk around—we'd take the little trail that led down through the trees to the beach. I decided to go out there by myself. I brought *Breakfast of Champions* with me.

It was a windy, gray day, so it wasn't as crowded as it could get on some weekend days. Just the more dedicated dog walkers and runners, who thinned out as I got farther from the parking lot. I walked down through the grassy fields under the old military buildings and entered the woods. By the time I got down to the beach, I practically had the place to myself. There was the usual bad smell from the sewage treatment plant nearby. The beach was littered with driftwood. I sat down on a sun-bleached log and looked out toward Bainbridge Island. A barge crept slowly across the horizon.

I read for a while but then my mind started wandering. And I don't know why, but I started thinking about this career test I'd taken when I was in seventh grade. They made you answer something like twenty multiple choice questions, and from your answers they could predict what you'd be when you grew up. The test predicted I'd be a dentist. My friends, who were going to be firemen or lawyers or politicians, all made fun of me. Dentist. It wasn't even the idea of looking into people's mouths—of bad breath and bloody gums—that got to me. It was the dentist lifestyle, and everything it implied. It was just too normal. Or worse than normal—mundane. At age twelve, it seemed like a fate worse than death.

For the most part, though, I'd always felt fairly hopeful when thinking about my future. Over the years I'd imagined all sorts of possibilities, from multi-millionaire business guy to rock star to expatriate journalist. But did I ever think I'd be in this kind of situation? Did I ever think I'd be this confused, this alone? Maybe I should've gone the dentist route.

The fucking phone rang. I looked at the back. I had figured out the whole caller I.D. thing and I saw that it was Chad. Fuck him. I didn't answer. I seriously considered throwing the phone out into the middle of the Sound.

I started reading *Breakfast of Champions* again. It had always been my favorite Vonnegut book. I don't know why. I was a big Kilgore Trout fan.

The phone rang again. An Oregon area code. My brother. This time I answered.

"Dude, what's up?"

"Not much," I said. "What's up with you?"

"Well, I got held up a bit. Some business I had to attend to."

My brother liked to refer to his "business." He thought he was being really cool.

He continued, "So I'm thinking it might take me a few more days to get out there. Maybe I'll be up there Wednesday. That cool?"

"Yeah," I said. "Fine."

"Dude, where are you? Sounds like you're in a vacuum or something."

"I'm at the beach."

Nick laughed. "You're such a nature boy."

"That's me," I said.

"Alright. Gotta go. I'll call you when I know what's up."

I hung up. Well, I didn't feel lonely anymore. Kind of the opposite of lonely. Harassed. Nick was like a hurricane that was off in the distance. You knew it was coming and there was only so much you could do to prepare. But in a way, I was looking forward to Nick coming. It would make life more interesting.

Chad wasn't around when I got back to the house. I was relieved.

I called Kelly. She seemed to be in a good mood and was up for the party. She had to get off the phone and go deal with the brats, so I told her I'd pick her up at nine.

After that I sat around brooding about the whole Chad situation. The more I thought about the previous night, the more pissed off I got. I wondered if Chad had called me earlier with some sort of task, or if he had called to apologize. Either way, I was thinking that we needed to have a little chat.

Chad came home after dusk. He walked over and knocked on my door.

"Hey, I tried calling you earlier. Was your phone turned off?"

"Oh," I said. "Whoops."

"Anyway, I wanted to apologize for last night."

"That's cool," I said. "Don't worry about it."

"Well, it's not cool. I don't want you to think I'm a total asshole."

I shrugged.

"Don't mention that Tanya girl to Melissa, okay?"

"I wouldn't."

Chad looked relieved. "Cool. Hey, I ordered a pizza. Should be here in about forty-five minutes if you want to join. Melissa is coming over, too."

"Sounds good."

"Okay, see you in a bit." He walked out and closed the door.

Well, so much for our "chat." I was such a fucking chicken.

Milo popped out of the couch. It seemed like Milo was never around when Chad came over.

"You don't like Chad much, do you?"

Milo just looked at me like I was an idiot. Then he bit me.

Right before I went over to the house, the phone rang.

"Hey, is this Kato?" It was Dan. I could hear Tammy giggling in the background.

"Hilarious," I said.

"Hear any weird thumps in the night?"

"Yeah, but your momma said not to tell you about it."

I heard Dan let out a breath. "Don't be talking shit about my mother."

"Sorry."

"You better be sorry," he said.

I heard Tammy say something in the background.

"What did Tammy say?" I said.

Dan was laughing. "What? Nothing. So what's the word?"

"Pizza," I said.

"You guys got pizza over there? Can we come over?"

"Fuck no. O.J. will kick your ass."

"Shit."

"What are you guys doing tonight?" I said. "Want to go to a party?"

"Hell no. We hate parties."

"Okay, never mind."

"Are there gonna be any good-looking chicks? Ow!" He was laughing and fumbled with the phone. "Tammy just hit me. Really hard."

"It's over on Capitol Hill." I gave him the address.

"Okay, we'll see you there."

"Good," I said.

Melissa greeted me when I walked into the house. I hadn't seen her since the night at the restaurant. Her whole manner seemed different this time—she seemed really, really mellow—kind of sleepy. She was wearing a loose sweater, and when she came over to give me a hug, I could tell that she wasn't wearing a bra.

"Hi Keith," she said. "How are you?" She was smiling like a maniac. Okay, she was definitely high.

"Great," I said. "Couldn't be better."

"You like living here?"

"Yeah," I said.

"That's really great." She laughed and shook her head and looked at the floor.

Chad walked in. "Keith, buddy, how you doing?"

"Good," I said.

"Hey, do you get high?"

"Uh, sometimes." I sure as hell didn't want to get high with Chad and Melissa. I didn't even know what drug they were doing.

"Is now one of those times?"

"I think I'll pass. Thanks, though."

"He doesn't like us," Melissa said, making a sad face.

"Aw, he likes us." Chad winked at me.

The doorbell rang.

"Oh shit, I just realized, I don't have any money," Chad said. "I hope they take credit cards."

Melissa rolled her eyes. "I've got it. Don't worry."

As she went to the door, Chad winked at me again. I decided that if he winked at me once more, I was going to kick his ass.

Melissa came back with the pizza. "Mmmm, smells good."

"What'd you get?" I asked.

"Mushrooms," Melissa said. And then the two of them started laughing really hard. There is nothing worse than hanging out with high people when you're sober.

For some reason, Chad didn't like eating in the kitchen, so we ate the pizza sitting cross-legged on the living room floor. Then Chad went and got some supposedly expensive French wine out of the basement. When he opened it, some got on the rug, and then there was a big discussion about what to do—cold water, hot water, baking soda, salt, whatever. Melissa ended up getting some paper towels and she and Chad mopped it up as best as they could.

After a while, Chad said, "Keith was asking about my dad."

"Really?" Melissa said.

"Yeah, he talked to Ed next door."

"Ohhhhh," Melissa said. She seemed kind of out of it. She was chewing her pizza really slowly.

Chad looked at me. "My dad was a great guy." He lifted his glass. "Here's to my dad."

"To your dad," Melissa said.

We drank to Chad's dad.

"Did you ever meet him?" I said to Melissa.

"No," Melissa said. "Never."

I looked at Chad for some explanation, but it didn't come. Instead, Chad said, "So what did Ed tell you?"

"He said that they used to play golf together."

Chad nodded. "My dad loved golf."

"He said that your dad was a pretty successful business guy."

Chad smiled. "Yes and no."

I didn't say anything.

Chad took another sip of wine. Then he said, "My dad's assets weren't in the greatest shape when I got them. A lot of people assume that I inherited a ton of money, but that's not true. When I sold his company, I was barely able to cover his debts."

Melissa and I just nodded.

"Like this house," Chad said. "He had two mortgages on it."

I glanced at Melissa, but I couldn't get a read on what she was thinking. Her eyelids were at half-mast.

"Anyway, I really miss him. I really do."

And that was that.

We were almost done with the pizza when Chad said, "Oh, by the way. I almost forgot but I'm going away on business tomorrow. Can you drive me to the airport?"

"Sure," I said.

"And hey, I was thinking we should have a party over here next weekend."

"A party?" Melissa said. She seemed to wake up a bit.

"Yeah, what do you guys think?"

"Yeah," Melissa said.

"Cool. Let's do it. Saturday night." Then he said, "Maybe we could get a band or something. Know of any bands?"

Chad was looking at me, so I said, "I know a band."

"Yeah?"

"I'm not sure you'd like their music."

"What kind of music?"

"Well, I think they're kind of rockabilly."

"Rockabilly? Cool! Definitely talk to them. See if they'd be interested."

"Okay," I said. "I can't guarantee anything."

"Don't worry," Chad said. "I trust you."

I got out of there as fast as I could after that. Suddenly, I didn't give a shit about Chad. Fuck Chad. Fuck Chad and fuck Chad's dad. I was thinking about Kelly. Mmmmmm, Kelly.

And Kelly was looking really good when I picked her up. She was wearing a short dress and these crazy shoes. They were black and sparkly and had huge heels. She could barely walk in them.

"Where'd you get those shoes?" I said.

"What? You don't like them?"

"I love them," I said.

"So who are these people?" Kelly said. "Are they nice?"

We were driving over to Capitol Hill and were stuck in the usual downtown traffic. She was sitting behind me with her arms around my neck. Her arms smelled good—like peaches.

"Work people," I said. "From my old job."

"I'm shy," she said.

"Don't worry, you'll like them. And Dan and Tammy will be there."

"Oh good," she said.

Sam was happy to see me. Not many people had arrived. I could tell he was impressed with Kelly.

"Did my friend Dan show up yet?" I said.

"I don't know," he said.

"You'd know," I said.

We walked into the living room. I recognized about half the people from work. And when I saw Don, sitting by himself on the couch, wearing yet another Hawaiian shirt, I started to regret coming.

Don jumped up the second he saw me. "Keith! How are you?"

"Good." Then I said, "Nice shirt."

He smiled. "It's a new one. Like it?"

"It's great," I said.

Kelly was just kind of looking around, amazed. She was clinging to my arm and shivering slightly.

I said, "This is Kelly."

"Hi Kelly," Don said.

Kelly said hi. She didn't really look at him.

The apartment reminded me of when Sara and I had first moved in together. It was easy to spot the things they'd bought together—the new rubberwood kitchen table, the new futon couch. I didn't look but I was sure there'd be a new double bed in the bedroom. I remembered going to the mattress showroom with Sara, remembered lying side by side on new puffy mattresses.

Sam and Cathleen joined us.

"So what's it like?" Cathleen said.

"What's what like?" I said.

"Freedom."

"It's great."

"I'm jealous," Sam said.

"No you're not," I said.

"Yes I am."

"No you're not. Otherwise, you'd quit, too."

Sam looked uncomfortable and I felt kind of like a dick.

And then Patrick sidled up to us. Patrick was one of the porn aficionados from my job the year before. He was friends with Sam. That's how I had heard about the job at Bonner. From Patrick.

"Hey," he said.

"Hi Patrick," I said.

Patrick nodded. He was short and skinny and wore baseball caps to hide the fact that he was going bald at twenty-five. Besides porn, he was into nitro-powered remote-control cars. I'd gone over to his place once and we had taken one out to the neighboring elementary school blacktop. After showing me how to work the controls, he let me take over. That car was fast—too fast for me. I brought it around in a wide arcing circle, and when it was heading back toward us at forty miles per hour, I got right and left backwards and steered it into a tetherball post. Patrick didn't take it too well.

Anyway, this was the first time I had seen him since we had worked together. He just kind of stood there, sipping at his beer and ogling Kelly. I'd never known him to have a girlfriend. The ogling kind of pissed me off. I was getting ready to say something when Dan and Tammy arrived.

Dan lived to crash parties. The fewer people he knew at a party, the more fun he had. I could tell right away that he was excited about this party.

"Yo, Kato!" he yelled across the room.

Kelly and Tammy squealed and started hugging each other. Dan rushed me and got me in a headlock.

"So what were you saying about my mother?" he said.

"Nothing," I said.

"I told you not to say shit about my mother."

"I'm sorry," I said.

"I can't hear you."

"I'm sorry," I said.

"Still can't hear you."

"I'm really really sorry!"

"Okay." He let me go. "So where's the beer?"

It went downhill from there. Dan had to introduce himself to everyone. And then more people came. And everyone got really drunk.

I knew it probably wasn't a good idea to drive, but it was past midnight, and Kelly was about to turn into a pumpkin. She was also getting kind of weird. I went to the bathroom and when I came back, I found her in the corner of the kitchen crying. When I asked her what was wrong, she just shook her head.

So I was more than ready to get out of there. I'd realized that I would be happy if I never saw any of those people ever again. Dan, meanwhile, was best friends with everyone. When I told him that we were leaving, he called me a party pooper—he and Tammy were going to stay.

I drove really slowly to Kelly's house. I was sober enough to be paranoid—I kept thinking about how I had been pulled over by the cop when I had Milo in the car with me.

Kelly was wasted. I could hear her mumbling to herself in the back seat.

We got to her house without a problem and I helped her inside. She slumped against the banister for a while and then slowly pulled herself up the stairs without even looking back at me. I closed the front door as softly as I could. I was about to get back in the car when Bob appeared.

"Keith?" he said.

"Yeah?"

"It's me. Bob."

"Bob. Hey."

"Are you drunk?"

"No."

"You're drunk. I can tell you're drunk."

"Oh," I said.

"You shouldn't be driving."

"Oh," I said.

"Here, I'll take you home. You can come back for your car tomorrow."

"Okay," I said.

"Let me just get my keys."

"Right," I said.

As soon as he went back inside, I jumped in the car and got the hell out of there.

When I got home, I checked my bumper for body parts. Then I went to bed.

Thirteen

Chad was banging on my door. "Hey Keith. Wake up! I'm gonna miss my flight!"

I had my face pressed into the pillow. No way was I getting up. But then the door opened.

"Hey Keith, wake up buddy."

As soon as I raised my head I was smacked between the eyes with a vicious headache.

"Ow," I said.

"Wow. You look like shit."

I put my face back into the pillow.

"No, no, no," Chad said, yanking at me. "Come on. I'll drive."

The sun was unbelievably bright in the Explorer. I slumped down in the passenger seat with my arm over my eyes as Chad drove too fast, swerving and honking and yelling at cars. I was sure we were going to die but I didn't care.

And then we were on I-5, doing ninety in the carpool lane.

After a while, Chad said, "I've got some Tylenol in the glove compartment if you want some."

"No thanks," I said.

"Always works for me."

"Yeah, and it makes your stomach bleed."

Chad didn't say anything for a while. Then he said, "You go out with Kelly last night?"

"No," I said. I didn't want to talk to Chad about Kelly.

"She's nuts. I meant to warn you about her."

I didn't say anything.

"You ever see her in one of her moods? Scary."

I still didn't say anything.

"But man, it can be worth the effort. I mean..."

"Shut the fuck up," I said.

"What?"

"I said shut the fuck up."

"I was just joking around."

"Yeah," I said.

"Sorry."

I put my arm back over my eyes.

The door slammed shut. When I opened my eyes, I saw that we were double parked at the gate and a rent-a-cop was whistling at me to move. Chad was trying to rush through the curb-side check in.

The fucking rent-a-cop kept whistling at me. I thought the whistle was going to drill through my head. I managed to climb over the center console and get into the driver's seat. I floored it out of there, almost running over several people in a crosswalk.

Chad had the seat adjusted way low and way far back. It was strange because I was taller than him. I was trying to get the seat adjusted and merge onto I-5 at the same time.

And then my phone rang. So now I was gonna be one

of those cell-phone-talkin'-SUV-drivin' assholes.

"Hello?" I said.

"I left my briefcase in the back seat."

I swerved across four lanes of traffic to the off-ramp. I was back at the airport pronto.

"Thanks," Chad said when I pulled up. "And sorry. I didn't mean anything about Kelly."

"Whatever," I said.

"Oh, and remember about the party. Talk to that band that you know."

"How much can you pay?"

"I don't know. Five hundred? Make whatever arrangements you want. I'm putting it in your hands." With that, he ran off toward the gate.

Before I could even put it in drive that same fucking rent-a-cop came up and started whistling at me. I gave him the finger.

I stopped at a 7-11 for coffee. I drank a coffee and then I drank a Big Gulp. Then I went to the bathroom and pissed for about an hour.

After that I felt much better. I wove through traffic—practicing my high-speed Ford Explorer/Firestone tire lane changes. I rocked out to a cheesy Aerosmith cassette I found in the glove compartment and looked down on all those poor schmucks in their Civics and Corollas. Yeah, this was America. Land of the brave and home of the free.

Kelly called right after I got home.

"Bob is really angry."

"What?"

"He's said he's thinking about calling the police."

"Why?"

"He said you were way too drunk to be driving. He gave me this huge lecture about it."

"Yeah, well, Bob's not your dad."

"You don't have to be an asshole."

"I'm an asshole?"

"You were drunk."

"You were drunk, too."

"Not as drunk as you."

"That's funny."

Silence. Then she said, "I want Milo back."

"Come and get him."

"I will."

"Fine."

"Fine." She hung up.

I called Kelly back a few minutes later and Bob answered.

"That was very irresponsible what you did last night."

"Yeah, yeah. Let me talk to Kelly."

"I don't think she wants to talk to you."

"What the hell is this?"

"I'm hanging up."

"You're hanging up? Oh, good for you."

He hung up.

After that I just lay on the floor for a while. The caffeine from the coffee and the Big Gulp was really pulsing through my system. I couldn't really think.

The next person to call was Dan. "Dude, that was fun last night."

"I'm glad you thought so."

"What?"

I told him about Kelly.

"I told you not to let her get drunk."

"When?"

"The first night you met her."

"Yeah, well, I guess I forgot."

So then I told him about her and Chad.

"Whoa," he said. "That's ugly."

"Yeah," I said.

"I'd cut bait on that one, buddy. Yow."

"Thanks for the advice."

"Hey, that's what I'd do."

"Noted." Then I said, "My bro is coming in this week."

"Does he know about the bike?"

"No," I said.

Dan laughed. "Man, you should just go make up with Sara. Hit rewind."

So then I told him about Sara and Beth.

Dan made a noise that sounded like a cross between a snort and a hiccup. I could tell he was trying not to laugh. Finally, he said, "Holy crap, dude."

"Yeah."

"Sheesh. You've had quite a week."

"Tell me about it." Then I said, "Hey, you think Ramcharger would be interested in playing a party over here?"

"I think they broke up."

"Think they'd get back together for five hundred bucks?"

"Yeah."

"Cool," I said. "Chad wants to have the party on Friday."

"That sounds like a rad party."

"Yeah," I said. "It's gonna be awesome."

And then Sam called.

"You make it home okay?" he said.

"I guess." I didn't feel like elaborating.

"That's good," he said. "Oh, I got a weird email from Patrick today."

"Yeah?"

"Yeah, he thinks Kelly is like a porn star or something."

"He thinks that about everyone."

"Well, he sent photos."

"And?"

"I don't know. It's hard to tell."

"Tell Patrick he's an asshole, will you?"

"Will do."

I sat around most of the day, recovering from my hangover and trying not to think about my fight with Kelly. Milo seemed hungover, too. He didn't seem to like his cat food much anymore.

"You okay?" I said. "You miss your mama?"

I was wondering if Kelly was really going to come pick him up. She didn't have a car, so I kind of doubted it. I was also getting somewhat attached to Milo. I wasn't sure I wanted to give him up.

It was a sunny day, so I went out in the backyard and

sat on a lawn chair. Sun was supposed to be good for you. Vitamin D and all that.

I saw Ed puttering around in his backyard, but he didn't make an effort to come talk to me this time. He just raised one arm in greeting. I waved back.

Whose story should I believe—his or Chad's? Probably both were true.

And what kind of business trip was Chad going on, anyway? He didn't even say where he was going. Maybe he wasn't even going on a business trip. It was probably all a big lie. He probably was just going to Vegas to play the nickel slots. Shit, he hadn't even paid me a dime so far. That cheap fuck.

I must have dozed off. When I woke up, Melissa was sitting next to me.

This was like the third Melissa I had met. And I liked this one the best—she wasn't high, and she wasn't dressed like a corporate slut sorority girl. Instead, she was wearing a yellow sun dress. She looked great.

"I'm so embarrassed," she said.

"What?"

"About how high I was last night. I don't normally get like that. I still don't feel quite normal. I had to call in sick this morning."

"Don't worry about it."

She just shook her head. "Chad get to the airport okay?"

I told her about Chad leaving the briefcase in the back seat.

She laughed. "That's totally Chad."

"Yeah," I said.

"So now you have the whole place to yourself."

"Yeah," I said.

"That should be nice. It's so nice here."

"It is."

And then we both laughed. It felt kind of like a conspiratorial laugh, like we were both in on this whole Chad scam.

"Well, I just came by because I left my purse. God I was high."

"You find it okay?"

"Yeah," she said, holding up a small handbag.

"That's good."

"It is. It's very good."

We both laughed again. And then we both got kind of embarrassed.

Then she said, "Hey, I should have you over to dinner before Chad gets back. What do you think?"

"Sounds good to me."

"What are you doing tomorrow night?"

"Nothing."

"Great. Why don't you come over around seven?"

"Good."

"You know how to find the houseboat?"

"Yeah, I think so."

"Good. See you then."

I watched her walk across the yard. She gave me a little wave before she let herself out the fence.

I sat back in my chair. Holy shit.

Fourteen

The sun was just starting to set by the time I arrived at the houseboat. I brought a bottle of wine with me. I didn't know shit about wine. I went to a wine shop and the wine guy asked me what I wanted, and I said something good. And he said how much did I want to spend, and I said not that much but enough. Then he said what are you going to be eating with it, and I said I had no idea. So he sold me a bottle of white wine with a picture of a duck on it for thirty dollars.

Melissa looked incredible. She was wearing a small black dress and these silver heels. And you could tell from her arms that she hit the gym. She was buff.

I had been wondering if it was going to be like the first time I saw her, or the second time or the third time. Well, it was like the third time, or even better.

I handed her the wine and she said, "Wow. This looks like a nice bottle. Should I open it now?"

"Sure," I said.

"I was just about to make some martinis."

"Let's do the martinis," I said.

She brought out a tray with a martini shaker and the glasses and everything.

"You weren't kidding around," I said.

Melissa just smiled.

To me, martinis have always been like mainlining alcohol. A rush. We drank two—too fast. Melissa had to take her shoes off, she was stumbling around so much.

We went out and sat on the deck. A wake came through and Twinkle Toes rocked up against the rubber tires on the dock.

"So why did your dad call you Twinkle Toes?"

She laughed. "I used to do ballet and gymnastics and all that stuff. I think that's how my dad likes to think of me—as his innocent little girl in a pink ballet dress."

So then Melissa told me about growing up in Colorado. She had been a major party girl—a ski bunny who later got her shit together. It helped that she had a rich daddy who made sure she got into law school. She kicked her coke habit and she did the work when she got there. We went back inside and she showed me some photos of the family ski trips at Telluride. Wow, 80s ski fashions were frightening.

"So now you're a big shot lawyer."

"That's right."

"What do you do exactly?"

She took a sip of her martini. "Well, I used to say that I defend evil against evil."

"Now what do you say?"

She smiled. "I defend evil."

And then she said she better deal with the dinner or it was going to burn and then we'd have to order pizza, and all she and Chad ever did was order pizza and she was sick of it. I asked her I if I could help but she said no so I slumped on the couch and watched her.

I hadn't heard from Kelly since she had threatened to come get Milo, and frankly, I didn't really care. The more I thought about her, the more I thought that the whole thing between us was a mistake. A mistake I'd gladly make again, but still a mistake.

And here I was, about to (hoping to?) make another mistake.

The dinner was awful. It was some kind of cheese soufflé or something. And the wine wasn't that hot, either.

"This is great," I said.

"You like it?"

"Mmmm. Really good."

"The wine is terrific."

"You think?"

"Yeah. It has a great nose. Kind of fruity or something."

We ate in silence for a while.

"So you like living on a boat?" I said.

"Yeah."

"You don't get seasick or anything?"

She laughed. "No, you get used to it."

"Sea legs," I said.

"Yeah, I have great sea legs."

We both laughed. Damn this was strange.

I went to use the restroom. Maybe the houseboat got hit by a wake or maybe I was just drunk, but I pissed on the floor and had to clean it up. Then I looked at myself in the mirror. My eyes were bloodshot and my nose was red. How could she be into me at all? I looked like a dork.

So it was inevitable. We were gonna have to talk about Chad. And I thought I had issues with the guy.

"He's like a little kid," Melissa said. "Someone needs to tell him to grow up."

We were sitting on the couch, drinking yet another bottle of wine.

I asked her about what Ed had said—about Chad inheriting all his dad's money and making a mess of everything.

"Chad and his father didn't get along. Chad's father always wanted him to join his business, but Chad didn't want to."

"What did his dad do?"

"Real estate. He built a lot of ugly apartment buildings. And a lot of them weren't built to code. He was always being sued for this or that."

"So Chad wasn't into it."

"No. He wanted to go to film school."

I laughed. "Film school?"

"Yeah, but he didn't last. Chad doesn't last at anything. He has a short attention span, and he gives up easily."

Melissa took another sip of wine.

"Chad kicked around LA for a while. I think he was taking acting lessons and working as a waiter and stuff. Later, he ended up in San Francisco and co-owned some kind of night club for a while. He moved back up here right after his dad died, and that's when I met him."

"How did you meet?"

"Bob. My firm did some work for his company, and I met Chad at a party at Bob's house."

"Bob."

She laughed. "Yeah. They grew up together. I don't like Bob to be honest. Chad sold his father's business and went into some weird venture with Bob. I think they made quite a bit of money. But now Chad has some kind of new project. I think he's put everything into that."

"What is it?"

"I'm not supposed to talk about it. Actually, I don't really know much. It's like a big secret or something. He thinks he's going to make a lot of money with it."

"Is that why he's out of town?"

"Yes, there were some people he needed to see in San Francisco."

"Mister big shot."

Melissa laughed.

"What I don't get is why is he so fucking cheap? How come he never has any money?"

She laughed. "Chad's always been weird about money. His father never helped him at all. Chad never had money until fairly recently. I guess old habits die hard."

Then she said, "But what is sad is that he really grew up alone. His dad was never around. His mom didn't pay much attention to him. He has some older sisters but they ignored him, too. Then there was the whole thing with almost dying."

I said that must have been scary, crashing a motorcycle at that kind of speed.

"Motorcycle racing?" She started laughing. "Is that what he told you? I hadn't heard that one. I don't think Chad has ever even been on a motorcycle. No, when he was in college, he jumped into the shallow end of a swimming pool drunk."

When she saw my face, she started laughing.

"He can be quite convincing. I don't think he ever really means to lie—maybe that's why he's so good at it. Like I said, it's like he's a little kid. Him and all his friends. They're like children."

I was thinking about the errand Chad had sent me on, about the weird guy with the Zippo lighter. I said, "Have you met Joey?"

She sighed. "Yeah, I've met Joey."

"What is the deal with that guy?"

"I don't know. And frankly, I don't want to know. Chad has some strange friends." Then she said, "I think Bob is the worst, though. With his weird wife and his screwy kids. And that's how Chad got involved with that Kelly girl."

I didn't know if Melissa knew about me and Kelly. I didn't say anything.

Melissa was shaking her head. "I feel sorry for Kelly. I think she has some real problems."

"What kind of problems?"

"Well," she said. "I probably shouldn't say since I don't know for sure."

"What?"

Melissa just shook her head. "She's just young and confused. And I think Chad took advantage of that."

I wasn't sure what she meant by that, but I didn't feel like I wanted to press it, either.

The phone rang. Melissa answered and then took the

phone into her bedroom and closed the door. I stayed on the couch, feeling bloated and drunk and tired. The soufflé had made me feel a bit ill, too.

The door opened a few minutes later. Melissa said, "That was Chad." Then she said, "I didn't tell him you were here."

And there it was again—that goofy conspiratorial feeling we had shared out on the lawn the day before.

She came and sat next to me and then we started kissing. We kissed for a long time.

At first I was aware of just how different this was than being with Kelly. It sounds tacky as hell but Melissa was a real woman. She didn't have to take the bubble gum out of her mouth or anything.

We stopped and laughed a little bit nervously.

"Are we really doing this?" I said.

I guess we were. She started taking my clothes off.

Melissa had a waterbed. I couldn't believe it. A waterbed on a boat. I was drunk and tired and the waterbed really fucked me up.

"Relax," Melissa said.

Afterward, we just sloshed around on the bed.

Melissa said, "Are you okay?"

I said, "Yeah." But I wasn't. I don't know why, but I felt like I was about to cry.

"You don't look okay."

I almost tried to explain it to her, but I couldn't explain it to myself. It had something to do with Sara and something to do with Kelly and something to do with Melissa, but I didn't know what exactly. I just felt sad.

Melissa said, "Do you want to smoke some pot?"

"Okay," I said.

She got out of bed and walked across to her dresser. I noticed that she had a tattoo of a butterfly on her butt.

She came back with a small ornate silver pipe and some great smelling pot. She lit it up and passed it to me.

I took a hit and held it for a long time. The stuff was potent. I blew it out.

She took a hit and passed it back to me.

"No thanks."

She blew out her smoke and laughed. "Everything in moderation, right?"

"That's right," I said.

She smiled. "I really like you."

"I like you, too."

She just smiled at me for a while. Then she said, "I didn't know what would happen when I invited you over, but I'm glad I did."

"I'm glad you did, too."

"I didn't mean it exactly like that," she said, laughing. "I'm not a total slut, anyway."

"I know what you mean."

And then I was wondering what she and Chad had talked about on the phone—and if that had anything to do with anything at all. I wondered if Melissa was getting Chad back for something, if this was all some kind of weird game. I didn't like games, wasn't very good at them. But to be honest, what was I doing? Was I getting back at Kelly for something? Was I playing a game, too? It was like a bad soap opera.

Melissa seemed to be having the same thoughts.

"I don't know what's happening with me and Chad. We got in a big fight that night that you had to go pick him up at the bar. He can be such an ass sometimes."

"Maybe we shouldn't talk about Chad," I said.

"Maybe you're right."

I decided I better come clean about me and Kelly. I said, "So you know about me and Kelly, right?"

Melissa just started laughing.

"I was wondering if you were going to say something. I knew about it already. Chad told me."

"Oh," I said.

"She is cute."

"Yeah," I said.

"Crazy," she said. "We're all crazy."

I ended up spending the night (I had planned for this possibility by leaving Milo lots of extra food). I couldn't really sleep, though. The rocking motion of the houseboat really messed with my mind. I also had the spins from all the pot and alcohol—I couldn't close my eyes.

I got up and walked back out to the living room and stood in front of the giant glass window. The lights of I-5 reflected off the water.

I thought about the events of the last week or so. I thought about Sara and the mess with Darryl and quitting my job and my parents and Chad and now this. Man, I was all over the fucking place. I knew I wasn't going to last with this Chad thing now. I'd shot myself in the foot—maybe I'd done it on purpose. Mostly, though, I missed Sara. I could feel it in the bottom of my stomach. Why? Kelly and Melissa were both totally hot. Was I stupid? What was my problem? Melissa was right. We were all crazy.

After a while, I went back to bed. Melissa slept pretty soundly. Her body was really hot. I put my hand on her side. She was like a furnace.

I heard my cell phone ringing the next morning. Melissa was already up, getting ready for work. She took the phone off the chair and handed it to me. I didn't recognize the number on the back. I said, "Hello?"

"Beyotch," the voice said. "Where are you?" It was Nick.

"Uh," I said. "In bed."

"Well get up," he said. "Shit."

After I hung up, Melissa came back out of the bathroom. She was all dressed for work. She looked like Melissa number one again.

"Who was that?" she said.

"My brother," I said.

"You don't look too happy," she said.

"Yeah," I said.

"Well cheer up," she said. She gave me a kiss on the cheek. "Stay as long as you want. Just be sure to lock the door when you leave."

Fifteen

Nick had spent the night over at Tony's house—I guess Tony was living in Seattle now, over on Capitol Hill. So I told Nick to come over to Chad's whenever he was ready. He said he was ready now, that Tony had shit to do. I hadn't realized that he and Tony were such early risers. I had to race him over to Chad's.

I got there about five minutes ahead of them. I heard them before I saw them—the huge subwoofers in the trunk of Tony's Impala shook the entire neighborhood. The Impala—all chrome and sparkly turquoise paint and tinted glass—sounded like it was going to vibrate apart. It was so low to the ground that it scraped the driveway when they pulled in.

Nick stepped out of the car like he was stepping out of a rap video, like he was stepping out of a limo at a movie premier. Brand new baggy clothing. Bleached hair and the new-looking baseball cap turned backwards. Bright white tennis shoes.

"Yo, wassup?"

He gave me a handshake that swung into a bear hug. I could feel something heavy swing against my hip. Something a lot like a gun.

Tony got out of the car with his pit bull. Tony was huge. He must have gained fifty pounds since I had seen him last. Fat face with little squinty eyes.

"Keith," he said.

"Hi Tony."

He just nodded at me. Then he looked up at the house. Nick was looking at the house, too.

"Wassup with this house, man?" Nick said.

"I don't know," I said. "It's a house."

"Fucking gay." Nick started laughing. Tony started laughing, too.

"Shit," Nick said.

Tony's pit bull was pissing on one of Chad's bushes. Tony started jerking at the chain.

"Yo, I gotta go," Tony said.

"Alright, man," Nick said. "Thanks for the ride."

"No worries."

Tony yanked the dog back into the car. "Come on, bitch!" He nodded at me before closing the door. "Later."

The deep bass started up again. Nick and I watched as the Impala pulled away.

"Fucking Tony, man," Nick said, shaking his head. "That guy is a trip."

Nick seemed to appreciate the house more once he stepped inside. "This place is the shit," he said.

He sat down on Chad's black leather couch and put his feet up on the coffee table.

"You don't think it's gay?" I said.

"Naw, not on the inside, anyway. The outside is kinda

whack." He was looking around—like he was casing the joint. "So you like living here and shit?"

"I've got a small apartment out back."

"Yeah? So where's the dude you're working for? I gotta meet this guy."

"He's on a business trip."

Nick raised his eyebrows. "So you got the place to yourself?"

"Yeah."

This seemed to really excite Nick. I didn't like the look on his face.

"And the dude's rich?"

"It's hard to tell."

"He looks fucking rich." He seemed to think about this for another second, then shifted gears. "So what's up with you, man?"

"Not much."

"Yeah? How 'bout the whole thing with Sara? I was thinking about that and I think she wasn't right for you, anyway. Uptight bitch."

"Don't call her a bitch."

"Whatever," he said. "Seriously, man. I wouldn't worry about her."

"I'm not."

"Good. That's good. What I like to hear."

With that he pulled out a pack of cigarettes and a lighter.

"Oh, what, you're smoking now?"

"Who are you, mom?" He lit up.

"You talked to the folks lately?" I said.

Nick blew out some smoke. "Man, Phil's been sweating me non-stop. Fucking pisses me off."

Nick had started calling his dad Phil. I think it was just another way of distancing himself. I don't think Phil appreciated it.

"Did you talk to him?" I said.

"Naw. Just mom. Talked to her last night. I guess they're going to Tibet or some shit like that."

"Yeah."

"Dude, what's up with that?"

"Beats me."

Nick shook his head. "Phil is whack, man. Let's not talk about them." Then he stood up. "Let's check your place."

"Alright," I said. "This way."

Nick was standing in the doorway of the mother-in-law. He didn't look very impressed. "I guess this ain't too bad."

"Thanks," I said.

"I mean, yeah, I don't know. So what do you have to do for this guy? You don't have to suck his dick or anything, do you?"

"Fuck you."

Nick was laughing. "Sorry."

"So far I've run a few errands, but mostly I think he just likes having someone around the house."

"You're like that dude, what's his name?"

My face started getting hot.

"That O.J. dude. What's his name?"

"Kato?" I said.

"Kato," he said, laughing. "That's it. You're like Kato."

"Yeah," I said.

"It's true." Nick couldn't stop laughing. "Kato, man. Holy shit. That's funny." Then he said, "You gotta get the hair going, man. The funky Kato hair."

At that point Milo climbed out of the couch. Tony jumped about three feet. "Oh shit. You got rats, man."

"It's not a rat," I said. I picked up Milo.

"What the fuck?"

"It's a ferret."

Nick didn't want to get close. He actually seemed scared. His shoulders were all tensed up.

"What's a ferret?"

"It's kind of like a weasel."

"Yeah, looks like a weasel fucked a rat. Where the fuck did you get that thing?"

So then I told him about Kelly. Nick seemed impressed.

"Damn, dude, you already hooked up with another lady? You're making your little brother proud."

I just shrugged.

"So come on. Is she hot?"

"Yeah," I said. "She's pretty hot."

"Nice going, bro." He came up like he was going to give me a pat on the shoulder, but then he looked at Milo and seemed to think better of it. "Keep that thing away from me." He shook his head. "Chicks have some weird fucking pets."

A cell phone rang. We both went for our phones. It was Nick's phone. He glanced back at me and then stepped outside. I closed the door behind him so Milo wouldn't bolt.

Milo wasn't looking so good. It seemed like he was losing some hair. And was he losing weight? He also seemed kind of lethargic. Maybe the cat food wasn't such a hot idea. I decided that I'd better call Kelly—see if she really was going to pick him up.

Luckily, Kelly answered the phone. She didn't sound angry at me anymore. She even apologized.

"I'm sorry about the other day. Bob was being such an asshole and I got kind of freaked out."

"That's okay," I said. "Sorry I got angry, too." And as I said this, I was hit with guilt over the previous night with Melissa. It was weird though—I'd been over at Melissa's less than an hour before, and I'd almost forgotten about it. That was probably Nick's doing—he had a way of overshadowing everything.

Then I told her I thought something might be wrong with Milo.

"What?" she said. "He's sick?"

"I don't know," I said. "I can't tell."

"You have to take him to a vet."

"A vet?" I said.

"Yes, a vet."

"Do vets look at ferrets?"

"Of course vets look at ferrets. I'd take him but I'm stuck here with the kids."

"I don't know," I said. "Maybe he'll get better."

"Yeah, or maybe he'll die."

I could sense she was getting really upset. I said, "Okay, I'll take him."

"Thank you," she said. "I'll make it up to you."

Nick walked back in a few minutes later. "Sorry about that, man. Business."

I was getting ready to tell him that we had to go to the vet when he said, "So where's my bike?"

I had rehearsed how I was going to say this, but I fucked up. I fucked up before I even said anything. Tony could see it in my face.

"What?" he said.

"Well," I said. "It's..." Then I said, "I think it got stolen."

"You think?" he said. "Dude, don't even..."

"I'm sorry," I said.

"You ain't shitting me?"

"No."

Nick didn't say anything for a moment. He sat down, took off his baseball cap and ran his hand through his hair. Then he put his cap back on and said, "So let me get this straight. You had my bike. My most prized possession in the whole world. And you let it get stolen?"

"I didn't 'let' it," I said. "'Let' isn't the right word."

"Well, did it or did it not get stolen?"

I almost commented that he sounded a lot like Phil right then, but I resisted the temptation.

"I think," I said. "I'm not sure."

"Oh, you're not sure. Well why don't you tell me what you are sure about?"

So I told him everything I knew.

Tony was just shaking his head. Then he said, "So who's this Darryl guy?"

"He's a baker."

"Yeah, well, he's gonna be one sorry motherfucking baker. That's all I can say."

"Don't do anything crazy," I said.

"I ain't gonna do anything crazy."

"What are you gonna do?" I said.

"For now, nothing. I gotta think." He shook his head. "This Darryl dude don't know who he's fucking with."

After Nick calmed down a bit, he seemed surprisingly willing to go to the vet. But he refused to hold the ferret. I went into the house and found a shoe box in Chad's closet. I poked a few air holes in the top and we put him in that.

When we walked out to the Celica, Nick said, "Don't even tell me this is your car."

"Okay, I won't."

"Shit, dude. You're scaring me."

"Where's your car, anyway?"

Nick had a heavily modified 5.0 Mustang that he was very proud of—almost as proud as he was of his bike.

Nick said, "It's in the shop. Needs a little body work."

"Oh yeah? Why's that?"

Nick just shrugged. "People don't know how to merge." Then he said, "Hey, where's the front seat?"

The vet waiting room spelled like ammonia. Green vinyl chairs from the early 70s. I had picked it out at random in the phone book. When I called and asked if they treated ferrets, they simply said "yes."

Nick and I sat down. Nick immediately struck up a conversation with some guy who had brought in a pit bull with a bandaged leg. Pretty soon they were laughing and swearing and giving each other high fives.

I was sitting next to a grandmother and her cat. She asked me what I had in the box. When I told her she said, "What's a ferret?" So I took Milo out of the box and she said, "Oh! He is cute!"

After about twenty minutes I was shown into a small room that also smelled like ammonia. The vet was a middle-aged lady with rose colored glasses and blue hair.

"Now let me see," she said. She looked at Milo and shook her head. She took his pulse and then shoved a thermometer up his ass. Milo's eyes bulged.

"Well," she said. "It's one of three things. It could be diet. It could be that he has a bad adrenal gland—which is common, especially when they get older. Do you know how old he is?"

"No," I said. Then I said, "What's the third thing?"

"Stress," she said.

We left with strict diet instructions. I was supposed to go to a pet store and buy actual ferret food. Who knew there was such a thing?

On the way to the pet store, Nick informed me that we had been invited to a party that night.

"Where?" I said.

"That dude in the waiting room. He said his friends are gonna be having a little get together."

"On a weekday night?"

"Yeah. It's an anniversary or something."

"What kind of anniversary?"

"I guess one of their homies got shot last year."

"Great," I said. "Sounds like fun."

Sixteen

The "get-together" was in a pretty sketchy-looking neighborhood in the Central District. The house next door to the party house looked like it had been hit by a firebomb. The party house itself didn't look all that hot—weathered paint, a sagging roof, and an overgrown lawn surrounded by a rusted fence. Across the street, some tough-looking Asian kids were standing around a lowered baby blue Acura with huge exhaust pipes and custom wheels.

"Watch out for those dudes," Nick said. "They'll fuck you up."

"Why are we here again?" I said.

"Dude, just chill."

I parked behind the Acura and we got out. A few of the Asian kids looked at us but no one said anything.

Tony was supposed to be meeting us there. Apparently, he knew some of these people.

We walked up to the house and then wove through a bunch of people sitting on the front steps drinking forty-ounce bottles of malt liquor. The rap music grew louder as we approached, and nearly bowled me over when we stepped through the front door.

It was stuffy and hot inside, but people were milling around in big down jackets (though a few people had removed their jackets to reveal wife-beaters and gold jewelry). The house was all creaking floorboards, ornate moldings and flowery wallpaper dating back to who knows when. A grand old staircase led up to a reddish glow and competing rhythms.

We found Tony in the living room. He was standing over in a corner with his pit bull. He smiled at us when we walked up. He and Nick did the handshake.

No one could hear anything over the music. Nick and Tony were just kind of grooving to the beat.

The whole place reeked of pot. Some fifteen-year-old girls in tight tank tops walked by. Nick and Tony smiled at each other. I was feeling very very old.

"So where's your friend?" I yelled in Nick's ear.

"Who?" he yelled.

"Your friend," I yelled.

"What?"

"From the vet office!" I yelled.

Nick just shook his head. I didn't know if he hadn't heard me, if he didn't know, or if he had no idea what I was talking about.

An acquaintance of Tony's walked up and they did the handshake and their pit bulls started fighting. They were laughing and pulling the dogs apart.

"I gotta piss," Nick yelled. He walked off, leaving me with Tony.

Tony and I didn't say anything. The fifteen-year-old girls paraded back through the room again. A bunch of guys in their twenties all watching them. I wondered when the gang rape part of the evening started.

A minute or two later I noticed a commotion in the next room. People shoving, then a circle forming as people crowded forward to see what was happening. Then I saw that Nick was at the center of it. He disappeared from view for a second, and then he emerged, ducking and pushing his way through the crowd of gawkers in the doorway. He glanced back and then ran up to me. "Let's get out of here."

"What?" I said. "What happened?"

But Nick was already running toward the door. Tony apparently was staying out of it. He just smirked.

"What happened?" I said again as we ran out the front door and down the steps.

"Some guy didn't like me talking to his girlfriend."

"Oh great," I said.

"He said he was gonna come back with his gun."

"Good," I said. "That's good."

We ran across the street to the car.

"Oh shit," Nick said. "Your car."

And then I saw it: the driver's side window of the Celica was smashed. The car also looked lower somehow.

Then I saw the blood—blood all over the dashboard, blood all over the driver's seat, blood all over the door. It seemed to emanate from the stereo, which had been pulled half-way out. Then I remembered: Carl's razor blades.

"Fuck," I said. "I can't believe this."

"Dude, they slashed your tires."

So that's why the car looked lower.

"Great," I said.

Nick was looking around nervously. "We gotta get out of here."

Before I knew it, he had pulled something that looked like a knife out of his jacket and was working on the door of Acura. A piercing alarm went off and the Acura's horn started honking and the lights started flashing.

"Nick, what the fuck?"

"Get in," Nick said. He was already in the car, leaning down under the dashboard.

I was frozen. I saw shadows moving, dark shapes rushing toward us.

"Get in!" Nick yelled.

I ran around to the other side and got in. When I shut the door, Nick hit the power locks.

"Nick, you're crazy."

Nick had ripped the steering column apart and was messing with a bunch of wiring.

And then we were surrounded. It was the Asian kids. They were pounding on the windows. I saw guns and knives. The car started rocking back and forth.

"Hurry," I said.

Nick didn't say anything. He was grimacing. I could see his teeth.

A second later, the dash lights lit up and the engine revved to life. Nick dropped the clutch and I was thrown back into my seat. A body rolled over the hood, hit the windshield like a wave and then shot off to the side.

A block later Nick was yelling and laughing and pounding on the dashboard.

"Holy shit! Holy fucking shit!" His voice always got really high and started cracking when he got excited. He coughed and cleared his throat and started yelling again.

I was still trying to get my seatbelt on. It was difficult because I was shaking violently. I realized that the alarm was still on. I mentioned this to Nick.

"It'll stop," he said. And it did.

And then we were just cruising down quiet streets. I noticed that the car had a very rough ride. My kidneys felt every pothole.

After a while, Nick said, "This is a pretty nice car. Maybe I should keep it."

I just looked at him.

He smiled. "Just kidding."

"You almost got us killed. You know that, right?"

"What?" he said. "Were you scared? Did you shit yourself?"

"I'm serious."

Nick was laughing. "It's good for you, man. Your life is too boring."

"Fuck you," I said.

Nick was shaking his head. "It's too bad she had a boyfriend, man. That chick was hot."

He pulled out a cigarette and lit up. I was still staring at him so he said, "Oh, okay, I'll roll down the window."

I was in a daze. I felt all clammy and I realized that I smelled bad. I stunk, actually—worse than Milo. I'd heard that fear could make you stink. Now I knew.

A while later, I said, "Where are we going?"

"Doesn't Dan live around here?"

"No," I said.

"Yeah, he does. Remember, we went over there last time I came to visit?"

It was true. I couldn't believe Nick remembered that. Maybe smoking pot doesn't mess with your short-term memory as much as some people think.

We pulled up in front of Dan's house.

"This is it, right?" Nick said.

"Yeah," I said, defeated.

"Cool. Let's ditch the car."

Nick drove around the block and parked it in front of a house with an American flag flying from the front porch. When we got out, Nick looked at the car and shook his head. "It's just not a very good color."

Dan, Tammy and Kelly were in the living room, watching *Caddyshack*. That was the only video Dan owned. I'd seen it about fifty times. We came in right at the scene where Bill Murray is getting ready to blow up the gopher with dynamite. He was singing his gopher death song.

"Hey Keith, Nick," Dan said.

"Wassup?" Nick said. He and Dan did the handshake/ bear hug thing.

Then Dan looked at me. "Dude, you don't look so good."

"Yeah," Tammy said. "You look pale."

"Don't worry about him," Nick said.

Dan introduced Nick to Tammy and Kelly.

Nick turned to me. "This is the Kelly?"

"Yeah," I said.

"Nice," he said. "I mean, nice to meet you." He bowed down and kissed Kelly's hand. Kelly blushed.

"What have you guys been up to?" Dan said.

"Not much," Nick said.

"Yeah, not much," I said.

"How's Milo?" Kelly said.

"He's stressed," I said.

"Stressed?" Kelly said.

"That's what the vet said. That or his adrenal gland is messed up." And as I said that, I wondered about my adrenal gland.

Kelly looked horrified. "What? Is he going to be okay?"

"I think so," I said. "It's probably just his diet. I was feeding him cat food. I got him some ferret food today."

"That's good." She looked slightly relieved. "Poor Milo."

Nick couldn't take his eyes off Kelly. He said, "That Milo is one cute rat."

Kelly punched him on the arm. "He's not a rat."

Nick looked at me. "I like her."

No one said anything for a moment. Then Nick said, "So where's this Darryl dude? I'm just dying to meet him."

"He's at work," Dan said.

"Lucky for him," Nick said.

"Now, you don't know for a fact he stole your bike," Dan said.

"I know. I just want to talk to him, is all."

"Right," Dan said, smiling. He had trouble taking Nick seriously.

That's when my phone rang.

"Hello?" I said.

"Keith?" It was Melissa.

"Hi," I said. I started walking toward the kitchen to get away from the others.

"I didn't hear from you. I was starting to wonder."

"Sorry. My brother's been here and I've been pretty busy."

"That was fun last night," she said.

"Yeah," I said.

"I feel weird, though."

"Yeah."

"Do you feel weird?"

To be honest, after the events of the last hour, I didn't know what I was feeling. I said, "Yeah."

"Are you okay?" she said.

"Not really," I said. "It's complicated."

"I know."

"No, I mean, it has nothing to do with you."

"Oh," she said. She sounded hurt.

"I didn't mean it like that."

"Then what do you mean?"

"I don't know," I said. "Can I call you back?"

"No rush," she said. And then she hung up.

I just stood there for a while, trying to figure out if I should call her back. No, I would only dig myself deeper.

In the other room, Nick had everyone in hysterics. At first I thought he was telling them about stealing the car, but then I realized it was some story about college. Something about locking someone in a trunk.

"Your brother is crazy," Dan said, laughing.

"I know," I said.

I could see that Kelly was watching Nick. Her eyes were big with wonder. And for the first time, I saw her for exactly what she was: a twenty-year-old girl from Sweden.

There was a knock at the door. Dan went and looked out the little peephole.

"Cops," he said.

My heart leapt into my throat. I turned just in time to see Nick dodge into the back room.

Dan looked at me. "What's up?"

I shrugged. I found that I couldn't move. My feet were bolted to the floor.

Dan hesitated a moment, then opened the door.

There were two cops. One of them said, "We have a report of some stolen property."

"Oh yeah?" Dan said.

"Can we come in?"

"Uh," Dan said. "I guess."

I couldn't believe Dan did that. Everyone who's ever watched *Cops* knows that if the police come to your door, you step outside and close the door behind you. In fact, Dan himself had lectured me about this once.

The cops walked in and started glancing purposefully around the room. They both had their hands on their hips. They had a shitload of equipment on those hips—guns, mace, nightsticks, handcuffs, walkie-talkies—and they looked fucking serious. Oh well. I was going to jail. Might as well give myself up.

One cop hitched up his pants and said, "We had a report of some wind chimes being stolen."

I couldn't help it. I burst out laughing.

"Is that funny?" the cop said.

"No," I said. "Sorry."

At that point Nick walked out of the back room. He acted surprised to see the cops. "Good evening, officers," he said in his best Eddie Haskell voice.

The cop looked at Nick for a second, then turned their attention back to Dan. "So you don't know anything about the stolen wind chimes?"

Dan shook his head. "Nope."

By now the other officer had noticed Ken's grow lamps. He walked into the kitchen.

Dan followed him, explaining, "My roommate is a horticulturalist."

The cop nodded. "I can see that." He started rubbing one of the leaves between his fingers. "I've got something of a green thumb myself, but your roommate is clearly talented."

"I know," Dan said. "We're all very proud of him."

After the cops had left, Dan said, "Fucking cops, man. Don't they have anything better to do?"

"I can't believe they came out because of the wind chimes," I said. "That was like two weeks ago."

"Well, actually..." Tammy said.

"What?" I said.

Tammy was looking at Dan. "Dan went on a bit of a spree."

"A spree?" I said.

"Yeah," Dan said. "Last night, after a few beers, I decided to rid the neighborhood of wind chimes."

Nick started laughing. "Awesome."

"Want to see?"

"Yeah," Nick said.

We followed him downstairs into the basement. There must have been about twenty wind chimes piled in the corner by the water heater.

"That's quite a collection," I said.

"What do you think I should do with them?" Dan said.

"Put them on eBay," Nick said. "You could make a ton of money."

"Yeah," Dan said. "Sure."

Later, Dan drove me and Nick back to Chad's place.

"Celica still having problems?" Dan said.

"You could say that," I said.

"The clutch?" Dan said. "I thought Carl fixed that."

"No," I said. "That's not it."

"So what's wrong with it now?"

"I think it needs new tires," Nick said.

"But it has new tires," Dan said.

"There was some sidewall damage," Nick said.

"Huh," Dan said. "That's strange. Bring it by tomorrow. Maybe we could warranty them for you."

"That sounds good," I said.

When we got back to Chad's house, Nick said, "So when does Darryl get off work?"

"Around eight," Dan said.

"Oh, okay," Nick said. "I'll try back tomorrow then."

Dan looked at me. I shrugged.

Seventeen

Chad called the next morning bright and early. He was at the San Francisco airport and was about to board a plane to Seattle. He asked if I could pick him up. I said fine.

Nick was sleeping like a baby on the floor. He had wanted to sleep in the house, but I didn't really trust him in there alone. Once during the night, he woke up screaming after Milo attacked his ear. I locked Milo in the closet.

I got up and let Milo out of the closet. He seemed to like the new food, but I couldn't tell if he was getting better or not. He still looked pretty bad. And he was pissed off about being locked in the closet. He started running around the room at warp speed. Within seconds, he was after Nick again.

"Ahhhh!" Nick said. "Fuck!"

I plucked Milo off Nick's chest. "Time to get up."

"Damn, dude." He sat up and started scratching himself.

"You have some major bed head," I said.

"Fuck you."

"When did you start bleaching your hair, anyway?"

"I don't know." He looked annoyed.

"You do that yourself?"

"Hell no."

"So you pay money for that?"

"Dude, just fuck off, okay?"

I was glad to know that I could still rile him up like when he was twelve.

Nick said, "I need a cigarette."

He got up and walked outside, wearing just boxer shorts and a t-shirt.

I made some coffee.

When I went outside with the coffee, he was sitting on the lawn chair, smoking and talking on his cell phone. His bare legs looked pale and thin.

When he hung up, he said, "Tony said that those Asian dudes are hella pissed. We should be careful."

"Oh good," I said. "Do they know who we are?"

Nick shrugged. "There's ways of finding anything out." He took a sip of the coffee and made a face. "Dude, this coffee seriously sucks."

"I have to go to the airport to pick up Chad."

"That's cool. Tony is gonna pick me up a little later."

"What are you guys gonna do?"

Nick shrugged.

"You're not going to go mess with Darryl, are you?"

"Well, I'm not saying we're not."

"So what are you going to do?"

"Kind of depends on Darryl, doesn't it?"

"Okay," I said. I didn't really care anymore. Then I remembered my car. "What should I do about my car?"

"Fuck if I know. You got triple A?"

"I think so." And then I remembered—Sara did. I had a card once but had lost it.

"Then let them deal with it. I wouldn't go back there if I was you." Nick smelled under his arm and wrinkled his nose. "Man, I stink. Can I use your shower?"

I took Chad's Explorer to the airport. How much had happened since I had dropped him off? Hmmm, let's see. I'd gotten in a fight with Kelly and then made up (or had we? I wasn't sure.). My brother had come into town and I'd been involved in a car theft. And oh yeah, and I'd slept with Chad's girlfriend.

I decided I'd better talk to Melissa. No one had called me since the night before, so I just dialed *69.

"I'm kind of busy right now," she said.

"Sorry," I said. "I just wanted to check in."

"Okay," she said.

"I'm on the way to the airport to pick up Chad."

"That's good."

"Hey, I'm sorry about last night. Things have been really crazy."

"Crazy," she said. "I know what you mean."

"I'm getting the feeling you're angry at me. I'm not sure what I did but I'm sorry."

"I'm sorry, too," she said. "Maybe we should leave it at that."

"Okay," I said.

Silence.

"Alright, well," I said.

"I should get back to work."

"Right," I said.

"See you around." And she hung up.

Well, to tell the truth, I was relieved. That definitely simplified things.

There was a horrible car accident on I-5 involving a big rig and about three cars that were literally crushed. I didn't know how anyone could have survived. I-5 was reduced to one lane and I was late to the airport. My cell phone started ringing as I went through the security check.

"Where are you?" Chad said.

"I'm almost there," I said. "I hit some bad traffic."

When I got to the gate, Chad was sitting in a chair looking impatient and dejected.

"Sorry," I said.

Chad didn't say anything. He just slung his bag over his shoulder and stood up. The bag pulled his shirt away from his "motorcycle racing" scar. I almost felt like saying something, but I didn't.

I ended up driving back. Chad looked tired.

I said, "So how was the trip?"

"Fine," Chad said.

"Get everything taken care of?"

"I guess."

I decided I'd better mention my brother. "By the way, my brother is in town. He's staying over for a few days."

"That's nice," Chad said.

Well, that was easy. So then I said, "So we still doing the party Saturday?"

Chad sat up a bit. "Yeah. You get that band yet?"

"I'm working on it," I said.

"Good. I'll talk to a caterer today. I've got a bunch of wine already, but maybe you should order a few kegs of beer."

"Will do," I said.

We pulled up to the house to see Nick riding around on his bike with a cigarette hanging out of his mouth. I can't say I was surprised.

"Is that your brother?" Chad said. He seemed to be more awake now.

"Yeah," I said.

"I used to race BMX. Before I raced motorcycles."

"Uh huh," I said.

We got out of the Explorer.

Nick pulled to a stop and said, "Sup?"

"You got your bike back," I said.

"Yeah."

"This is Chad," I said. "Chad, Nick."

"Wassup?" Nick and Chad shook hands.

"Nice bike," Chad said.

"Thanks."

"So Darryl gave you your bike back?" I said.

"Yeah," Nick said. "He said it was a misunderstanding. He felt kind of bad about it."

"What did you do to him?"

"Nothing," Nick said. "You know, we just talked."

"What happened?" Chad said, laughing.

"Someone stole his bike," I said.

"And you got it back?" Chad said.

Nick shrugged. "Yeah. You know."

"I like that," Chad said. "You'd be a good businessman."

"I already am," Nick said.

"Oh yeah? What's your line of business?"

"Ummm," I said.

"Import, export. You know."

"Oh," Chad said, nodding. "Right. Hey, we should talk later."

"Cool with me," Nick said.

I was just shaking my head. I couldn't believe any of this. Nick started circling around on his bike, popping wheelies, doing tricks and generally showing off. Chad looked really impressed. I walked inside.

I called Sara to get the AAA card number. She sounded a bit suspicious, but she gave it to me anyway. Then, I don't know why, but I invited her and Beth to Chad's party. She said she'd try to make it.

I called AAA. I told them where the car was and that I wanted to get it towed to Big Bob's. The operator asked if the keys were in the car.

"No," I said. "But the door's open."

Then I called Dan and told him what to expect.

"Cool," he said. "We'll find some tires for it."

Chad disappeared in his Explorer, so Nick and I took the bus down to Big Bob's. Nick looked extremely put out to be riding public transportation. It had started raining lightly, and the bus was all steamed up and putrid smelling.

"This sucks," he said.

"Yeah, well, whose fault is it that I don't have a car?"

"Whatever." Then he said, "Chad doesn't seem so bad. I was expecting a total dork."

"Well, you don't know him very well."

The Celica had new—or almost new—tires on when we got there.

Dan said, "Dude, you didn't tell me about the stereo thing."

Carl was there, laughing his ass off. "I love it, I love it."

"I don't know," Dan said. "Seems fucked up to me. Bad Karma or something."

"Please don't say that," I said.

"What?" Nick said. "You don't believe in that kind of shit, do you?"

"I don't know," I said. "I might."

"It ain't Karma," Carl said. "More like simple cause and effect."

"Exactly," Nick said. He was looking at all the blood and shaking his head. Then he said, "I'm just glad I don't have to clean that up."

"Oh yeah?" I said. "Who's going to do it?"

"Easy," Nick said. "Just take it to a detailing shop. Those guys know how to deal with blood. I've done that a couple times."

Everyone stared at Nick.

"Actually, there's a place right near here," Carl said.

I pulled the Celica in behind a row of BMWs and Land Rovers. A guy in a red polo shirt walked out holding a clipboard.

"Can I help you?"

"I want this fully detailed," I said.

The guy looked at the car and then looked back at me. "Is this a joke?"

"No joke. I want the full treatment."

The guy didn't say anything. Nick was giggling.

"I'm in a bit of a rush," I said. "How long will it take?"

Nick and I ate at the McDonald's across the street while the car got cleaned and waxed and whatever else. I watched Nick inhale three cheeseburgers.

"What?" he said. "I'm hungry. You didn't feed me any breakfast. You're a shitty host."

"Sorry." Then I said, "So where was the bike?"

Nick smiled. "In his van."

"In his van," I said.

"Yeah, he said he just wanted to borrow it. He said he was fucking around and then crashed it by accident. He said he was gonna fix it and give it back but then you pissed him off."

"He said that I pissed *him* off?"

"Right."

I shook my head. "So is it fucked up?"

"Naw. Just tore one of the grips and ripped up the seat a bit. That's all."

"So what did you do?"

"Nothing."

"Seriously. What did you do?"

Nick just shrugged. "Don't worry man. I'm not a total monster. Everything is cool."

After the detailing shop got done with it, the car looked fantastic. I almost didn't believe it was the same car. They tried to charge extra for the blood, but I managed to talk them back down by pointing out that they had to deal with one less seat. Still, it cost me close to half what I'd paid for the car.

As we drove back to Chad's, I said, "I should have done this earlier."

"Yeah," Nick said. "Now you just need a new window."

We spent the rest of the day hanging out at Chad's house. I made party preparations. I called and ordered the kegs of beer. Then I actually managed to talk to someone in Ramcharger—Lenny, the drummer. He sounded pretty excited, said sure they could play a gig, no problem.

When Chad got back he ordered a pizza. Then he and Nick proceeded to get drunk on wine. They started smoking cigars. Then Nick got his bike and started doing tricks in Chad's living room. Chad was laughing, egging him on. I was the third wheel. After a while, I decided to go back to my place and call Kelly.

Kelly wasn't feeling very talkative. We discussed Milo a bit and then ended up just saying we'd see each other the next day or at the party.

After that I read *Cat's Cradle* some more. Actually, I was feeling pretty good. For the first time since I'd moved out of Sara's, things seemed somewhat under control.

I was starting to doze off when Dan called.

"Dude, Keith," he said.

"What's up?" I looked at my watch. It was almost midnight.

"The bakery just called. Darryl didn't show up for work."

"What?" I said.

"Yeah, and he's not here, either. But the weird thing is his van is parked out front."

"Huh," I said.

"What did your bro do?"

"I don't know," I said.

"Well, you better find out."

"Okay," I said. "I'll try."

Nick and Chad weren't in the house, but I heard some whooping and laughing outside. I went out front to see Nick on the roof with his BMX bike. Chad was standing in the driveway yelling encouragement.

"What the hell are you doing?" I said.

"It's called a wheelie drop," Chad said. He was giggling manically.

"A wheelie drop?" I turned and looked up at Nick. "Where are you going to land?"

Chad was laughing. "On your car."

"Wha..?"

Just then, Nick launched off the top of the roof. It was like it happened in slow-mo. It really was a perfect drop. There was a horrible thud as Nick landed right on the roof of my car. He rolled down the windshield and hopped gracefully off the hood.

The roof of my car had a huge dent in it.

Chad was laughing and clapping. "Bravo, bravo!"

Nick did a little victory lap, pumping his fist in the air.

"What the fuck?" I said. "My car."

Nick pulled up with a big grin on his face. "Sorry dude."

"Right," I said. I got in the Celica. The roof was literally sagging.

"Maybe we can push it back out," Nick said.

Chad was shaking his head. "Fantastic."

I pushed on the roof a bit but then gave up. Then I looked at Nick. "Dan just called. He said that Darryl's missing."

"That's weird," Nick said. "He was at the house when we left."

I didn't say anything. I just stared at him.

"What?" he said.

Eighteen

The next morning, Ramcharger found Darryl hogtied in the basement. From the way Lenny described it, he was almost frozen—at first they thought he was dead. But as soon as they untied him, he jumped up and bolted to the bathroom.

Afterwards, Dan tried to talk to him, but he stayed in his room with the door closed for a long time. Then he left the house.

When I confronted Nick with this, he just shrugged. "What did you want me to do?"

"He could've died," I said.

"What?" Nick said. "No way."

"What if there had been a fire or something?"

"Whatever," Nick said. "And if he hadn't been tied up, he could have been run over by a bus. Maybe I saved his life."

"You're insane," I said.

"Believe me, he got off easy. You should have heard some of the sick shit Tony wanted to do."

"I don't want to hear about it." Then I said, "I'm sure he's going to do something crazy now."

Nick laughed. He spread out his arms like he was Ice Cube in *Boyz N the Hood*. "Hey, bring it on, man. Bring it on. I ain't going nowhere."

Actually, Nick was going somewhere—he was taking the ferry over to see the parents. He had talked to mom, and she had told him she would be really hurt if he didn't at least stop by. So he had agreed to go—he'd stay the night but would be back for the party.

"No way I'm gonna miss the party," he said. "That Chad dude is hilarious."

After I dropped Nick at the ferry terminal, I got a call from Chad. He wanted me to go to Georgetown again to pick up another one of those envelopes.

So I drove back down to the warehouse. After ringing the buzzer and staring up at the security camera again, Joey came to the door. He was looking pretty bad—his eyes were all puffed up and red. He was either sick, had allergies or was stoned—or all three.

He handed me the envelope. "I hear Chad's having a party tomorrow."

"Yeah."

He started rubbing his eye. "I might try to make that."

"Cool." Then I said, "You get your lighter back?"

"What?" He was rubbing his eye harder now—like he was going to gouge the eyeball out of the socket.

"The Zippo? Last time I was here, you left it on the hood of my car when you ran inside for a phone call. I put it on the loading dock."

Joey stopped rubbing and started blinking rapidly. His eye was tearing up pretty bad.

"You okay?" I said.

"Yeah," he said. "Fucking contacts."

"So I guess you didn't get the lighter."

"Nope." He shrugged. "Doesn't matter. I got a bunch of 'em."

"Were you in Vietnam?"

"What? You mean am I a vet?" He laughed. "Hell no. I go to Vietnam from time to time on business. They sell them on the street. They say they got 'em off dead GIs but it's bullshit. They're not even real Zippos. They're brand-new fakes but they make 'em look old and everything. It's a whole fucking cottage industry." Then he said, "Here, I got another one."

He handed it to me. This one said, WHEN I'M DEAD AND IN MY GRAVE NO MORE PUSSY WILL I CRAVE.

He laughed. "Pretty good, huh?"

"Sure," I said.

"You want it? You can have it. I got tons of 'em."

"That's cool." I tried to hand it back but he wouldn't take it.

"No, no. It's yours. Keep it."

I didn't really want it but I said, "Okay. Thanks."

I went back and sat in the car. This envelope wasn't as heavy, and it wasn't taped shut like the last one. So I opened it. Inside, there was a CD.

I had to find out. I drove over to Bonner to see Sam.

Bonner looked the same. It was weird to think that it had been less than two weeks since I had quit. It seemed like it had been months or years. I waved hello to the cute blonde receptionist with the nose ring. It looked like her infection had healed.

Luckily, I saw Don before he saw me. I had to dodge around a cubicle—I actually ducked down as he walked past.

Sam had his headphones on. He was in a zone, typing away like a maniac. He looked pretty surprised when he finally noticed me. He took off his headphones and spun around in his chair.

"Keith!"

"Hey Sam, what's up?"

"Nothing. What's up with you?"

"Not much."

He laughed. "So what are you doing here? You come to get your old job back?"

I shook my head and pulled out the CD. "I got something I want to check out. Mind if we pop it into your computer?"

Sam frowned. "It's not gonna give my computer some skanky virus, is it?"

"It might."

Sam shrugged. "Fuck it. I got all my shit backed up."

We popped the CD in. Image files. Sam clicked on the first one and the image opened onto the screen.

After a moment, Sam said, "Wow."

"Yeah," I said.

I'd seen plenty of porn over the years, but this was different. It's not that this was really special or new, it's just that, well, maybe it had to do with the resolution or something. High production values.

And then I recognized the girl—it was the girl I'd seen in the new BMW when I went down to Georgetown the first time. But this time, she was only wearing long white gloves and knee-high boots.

Sam opened a few more files. Each image was a slight variation on the previous image. It was like they were movie stills or something. Except that the point of view seemed to move, too.

"Um, yeah," Sam said.

"Okay," I said. "That's enough."

Sam popped out the CD and handed it to me. "Where did you get this?"

"Nowhere."

"Mind if I burn I a copy?"

I smiled. "Do you still have that e-mail Patrick sent you after the party?"

"Let me see." Sam went through his email files. "Here you go."

He opened the email. It read: "Sam, check this out. The password is TWINKLETOES."

"Uh," I said. "How did Patrick get the password?"

Sam shrugged. "He's a hacker."

"And how did he find this site?"

"You know Patrick. Porn is his hobby."

Sam clicked on the link that Patrick had provided and typed TWINKLETOES the password box.

The site took a second to load. It didn't look like an actual porn site. There weren't the usual flashing banner ads and links. And it was obviously still under construction.

"That her?" Sam said. He turned and looked at me.

I nodded. It was Kelly alright. Every inch of her. But it was hard to tell—the emphasis wasn't exactly on her face. Patrick was an observant fucker.

Sam clicked through a few images. There was a certain resemblance to the images from the CD in terms of the angles and setup, but they weren't quite as polished looking. Less glam, more raw.

"Check this out," Sam said. He moved his cursor over Kelly and Kelly started to move. By moving the mouse faster, Sam made her gyrate. He made her contort into various positions.

"Cool, huh?"

Just then Cathleen walked up. Sam wasn't able to close the window in time.

Cathleen put her hands on her hips in mock scorn. "What disgusting filth are you two looking at?"

"That's not filth," I said. "That's my girlfriend."

I drove back to Chad's. I couldn't get the little gyrating, contorting Kelly out of my head.

So this was the "new project" Melissa had mentioned—one of the pies Chad had his fingers in. I guess it was going to be some sort of high tech, interactive deal, and Kelly had been his BETA version. I shook my head. Chad. What a guy.

Mostly, though, I felt confused. I didn't know whether to be angry or not. I mean, what did I care if Chad was a porn king? But what about Kelly? I didn't know her too well, but it didn't seem like her kind of deal. I wondered if Chad had forced her into it somehow. And then I remembered what Melissa said a few days before: "She's just young and confused. And I think Chad took advantage of that." And what did Melissa know about it?

When I got back to the house, the Terrapin Cleaning Services van was parked out front.

Josh shut off the vacuum when I walked inside. "Hey," he said.

"How's it going?"

"I hear there's a big party tomorrow."

"Yeah," I said. "You coming?"

He shook his head. "No."

"Why not?"

He shrugged. "Chad didn't invite me." He looked kind of bummed.

I said, "Yeah, well, it's probably gonna suck anyway."

Josh shrugged and turned the vacuum back on.

The mother-in-law was filled with sun but somehow that just made it look bleak and barren, not warm. I walked over to the window. Those dead flies were still on the floor. I counted them again. Now there were ten of them.

Milo walked up to me and started sniffing at my shoes. He was looking better now, no question. I picked him up. "Hey little dude," I said. "Let's call your mom."

Then I dialed Kelly. I wasn't going to ask her about the photos or anything like that. I just wanted to talk to her, see how she was doing.

I got Bob instead. "She's out," he said.

"Can I leave a message?"

"Sure," Bob said, like he didn't mean it.

"Just tell her to give me a call when she gets the chance."

Bob didn't say anything.

"Got it?" I said.

"Sure," Bob said.

Right after that, Dan called.

"Darryl knows about the party," he said.

"What?"

"I thought I should warn you."

Somehow I didn't care. I said, "How did he find out?"

"I think Lenny told him."

"Well, that should be interesting."

"Yeah," Dan said. Then he said, "Your brother is nuts."

"Tell me about it."

"It's like he thinks he's living in a Tarantino movie or something."

"Or something," I said.

"You sound like you're in a shitty mood."

"That's cause I am in a shitty mood."

"I guess I can understand that," Dan said.

I suppose I could have told him about the porn site, but I didn't feel like it. I didn't know what else to say, so I said, "You coming to the party?"

Dan laughed. "You know it."

After Dan hung up, I sat back on the hide-a-bed and stared at the ceiling. I started thinking about Kato. What did Kato think about O.J.? Did Kato know what a shit O.J. was before the murders? Did he know what O.J. was capable of? Did he care?

And what about Nick Carraway? Hc knew that Gatsby was a crook. But maybe he was in denial about it or something. But then Gatsby was a compelling and sympathetic character. Chad wasn't. Chad was an asshole.

And then I thought about the other Kato. Not Kato Kaelin but the "real" Kato. Kato on the Green Hornet, played by Bruce Lee. I remembered watching him when I was a kid in San Lois Obispo—sitting cross legged in front of the TV on our orange shag rug. The real Kato kicked some serious ass.

So who was I gonna be? Kato Kaelin the loser? Or Kato from the Green Hornet—the kick ass Kung Fu fighter?

When Chad got home I walked over with the envelope. I could have just left it on his desk like the last time but I wanted to see if he betrayed anything when I handed it to him.

Melissa was in the kitchen, flipping through a magazine. She said, "Hi Keith," and smiled thinly.

"Hi Melissa," I said.

"How are you?"

"Good. Yourself?"

"Oh, fine."

She kept paging through the magazine—somewhat aggressively, I thought. It sounded like she was going to rip the pages out.

Then Chad walked in.

"Keith," he said. "You got the envelope."

"Yeah," I handed it to him. No reaction. He was totally blasé about it. But he didn't really look at me, either.

I looked at Melissa. Nothing.

"So I think we're all set," Chad said.

"Set with what?" I said.

"The party," he said.

"Oh, right," I said.

Chad looked at Melissa. "Are you ready?"

"Yup," Melissa said, standing up.

Chad turned back to me. "We're going out. I'll see you later."

"Okay," I said.

With that they turned and walked out of the room. I pictured a perfect Bruce Lee kick to the back of Chad's head.

I made myself some food. I played with Milo. Then I tried Kelly again.

Bob answered. "She went to bed early."

"It's eight o'clock," I said.

"She said she was tired."

"You didn't give her the message, did you Bob?"

"Might have slipped my mind," he said.

"You know," I said. But then I didn't know what to say. It wasn't worth it.

"What do I know?" Bob said.

"Nothing," I said, and hung up.

Later that night, Sara called. She said she was just "checking in" to see if I'd gotten the car towed okay, but I knew her well enough to know that something was up.

"So, how are you?" I said.

"Oh," she said. "Okay."

"How's Beth?"

Sara laughed. "Well, we just had our first fight. About you, actually."

"Really?" I said.

"Yeah," she said.

"So things..."

"I don't know," she said. Then she said, "I miss you."

"I miss you, too."

"Funny," she said. Then, "I know I shouldn't say this."

"No," I said.

"I mean, we just broke up, right?"

"Right."

"When we were together, seems like all I could think about was the bad stuff. Now all I can think about is the good stuff."

"Same."

"Really?"

"Yeah."

She didn't say anything, but it sounded like she was crying.

"Don't cry," I said.

"Okay," she said.

That night, I lay awake. I thought about my brother at home, arguing with Phil. I thought about Darryl seething at the bakery, plotting his revenge. About Kelly asleep in Bob's house, in that little single bed. About Chad arguing with Melissa. And I thought about Sara, in bed with Beth—thinking about me?

Then I thought about the conversation I'd had with Dan a few days before—when I told him about Chad and Kelly, about Sara and Beth. Could I hit rewind like Dan had said? My conversation with Sara made it seem like this was a possibility. But for the first time since I'd moved out, I knew that I didn't want to.

I realized that I'd been hanging around, waiting for my head to clear on this, and now that it had happened, well, I wanted to cut bait, disengage. I was ready to move on.

Nineteen

I picked Nick up from the ferry terminal at noon. He didn't want to talk about his night with the parents. All I could get out of him was, "Fucking bullshit, man."

The caterer's van was parked out front when we got back to Chad's house. They were unloading all sorts of fancy-looking food and had already set up a white tent in the backyard.

Nick started eating stuff right off the trays. The head caterer, an uptight, finicky guy with a little mustache, reprimanded him.

"Dude, come on," Nick said. "What's the deal?"

"Wait for later."

"But I'm hungry now."

"Well too bad."

Nick made a face, then grabbed two more small quiches and shoved them in my mouth. "Mmmm," he said. "Good."

The caterer just shook his head.

Melissa and Chad appeared later to see how things were going. They were both dressed up already—Chad in a shiny, Euro-style suit and Melissa in a little black party dress.

Nick seemed pretty blown away by Melissa.

"Hi," he said. "I'm Nick."

"Oh," Melissa said. "The stunt man."

"That's right."

"Very impressive."

Nick acted all modest. "Yeah, you know. I got a few tricks up my sleeve."

"I bet you do."

"Damn, she's hot," Nick said to me after Melissa had walked away. "I don't normally dig older women, but wow."

"Uh huh," I said.

"So she and Chad..?"

"Yeah," I said.

"Shit. All the hot bitches in Seattle are taken."

Two guys from Ramcharger pulled up in a battered pickup and started unloading equipment. They wheeled in the amps on little dollies and carried in the drums and cymbals.

Nick went over to talk to them and after a while I heard laughter and they all started high-fiving each other. From the sound of it, Nick had confessed to the Darryl thing. I guess the Ramcharger guys didn't like Darryl much, either.

After that Tony came by—decked out in full Charlotte Hornets sweats—and then he and Nick disappeared on "business."

Chad's friends started arriving around dusk. Soon cars were parked all the way down the block.

It was a bigger crowd than I had expected. Mostly people around Chad's age, mostly well-dressed, and mostly white. And everyone seemed to know each other. Clumps of people formed here and there, laughing and spilling their drinks onto the lawn. Chad moved from group to group with Melissa in tow.

Bob and his wife appeared meekly behind a wave of guests who were obviously already drunk—laughing and waving and yelling. Bob's wife had the Bride of Frankenstein look going again. Bob just scowled at me as he made a beeline to the hors d'oeuvres.

Dan arrived with Tammy and Kelly a bit later. Tammy seemed impressed by the house. She kept saying, "Wow." We all went to hide out in my place for a while.

When Dan saw my mother-in-law, he said, "Super Kato style."

Kelly rushed over to Milo, picked him up and clutched him to her chest. She started petting him furiously. "Oh my poor baby. My poor baby. Momma isn't going to leave you again."

I said, "I called you a couple of times yesterday."

"You did?"

"Yeah, I guess Bob never gave you the message."

She shook her head. "I thought you were mad at me or something."

Tammy was looking vaguely embarrassed. I wondered if they had been talking about me.

To change the topic, Tammy said, "I can't believe what your brother did to Darryl."

"What did he do?" Kelly said, wide-eyed. When they told her, she just got more wide-eyed. I couldn't tell if she was upset or impressed or both.

I turned to Dan. "You seen Darryl today?"

Dan smiled. "Nope. His van was gone, too."

"Great."

Outside, there was a burst of feedback and then someone from Ramcharger was saying, "Test, test."

Dan laughed and shook his head. "Those guys suck."

It was funny to see Chad's friends crowded around Ramcharger while they played. The Ramcharger guys were acting like a bunch of rock stars—like they were playing the Tacoma Dome, not in front of a bunch of middle-aged losers.

The worst thing about Ramcharger was their lead singer—Rick. The guy was an asshole. He thought he was Iggy Pop or something. Scrawny and heavily tattooed, he liked to take his shirt off and writhe around and pretend to fuck the microphone stand.

Rick was the one who was always trying to change the direction of the band—always trying to figure out how to capitalize on the latest music fad (hence the recent switch to rockabilly). He didn't show up until the last moment, and then he didn't really seem into it. He wore a big cowboy hat and leather pants and kept his back to the crowd. Every once in a while he'd drop the mic, fall onto the ground and start writhing around—kind of postmodern, rodeo inspired break dancing. They obviously hadn't rehearsed for a while, and the songs all seemed longer and looser than I remembered. I'd only seen them play once in a pizza joint and that was a year or two before.

Meanwhile, Chad realized that he hadn't bothered to warn the neighbors, so he rushed around and invited them all at the last moment. After the music started, I saw Ed walk out into his backyard and shake his head. The people in back weren't home. That left the big house on the other side and Chad was only able to talk to the housekeeper, who didn't speak English.

Later, Chad came up to me and said, "Great band."

I couldn't tell if he was serious or not. I said, "Yeah."

One woman was doing some kind of trance dance around the band. She was wearing a pink feather boa which she kept wrapping around Rick's neck.

Chad said. "Thanks for all your help."

"No problem."

And for the first time in a while, Chad didn't seem like such a bad guy. Suddenly I didn't care that he owed me money, that he had been a dick half the time, that he had some rather shady business dealings. And I was sorry that I had slept with his girlfriend.

I was pretty amazed when Sara and Beth walked up. Ramcharger had just finished a set, so we could actually hear each other.

"Great band," Sara said, and rolled her eyes. She was wearing a red leather jacket I had never seen before. Then I realized that it was Beth's.

"Hey," I said. "Thanks for coming. You look great."

"Thanks," Sara said, smiling. "So do you." Then she said, "Thanks for inviting us. It was very nice of you."

Beth looked like she was going to throw up.

"So you live here now?"

"Yup."

"It's nice," she said.

"It's okay," I said.

"Who are all these people?"

"I don't know. Friends of Chad's."

"And where's Chad?"

I pointed to Chad, who was standing by the caterer's tent, talking to Bob. I said, "See those two guys over there?"

"Yeah."

"Chad's the one who isn't fat."

"Oh," Sara said. "Right."

"What does he do?" Beth said.

"He's a pornographer," I said.

They both just looked at me. And that's when Nick and Tony arrived on the scene.

"Yo," Nick said.

"Hi Nick," Sara said.

"Hey," Nick said, guardedly. Then he shot me a look.

"How's school?" Sara said.

"Oh, you know. It is what it is."

Sara laughed. "That's very profound."

Nick frowned. "Whatever."

Tony's pit bull was sniffing at Beth. Beth said, "Get that dog away from me."

Tony pulled his dog back and said, "Sit."

After a while, Nick said, "This party sucks. We should start some shit."

"Yeah," Tony said.

"What are you going to start?" Beth said.

Nick looked Beth up and down but didn't answer. Then he looked at Tony and said, "Come on."

The two of them walked off toward the food.

"Charming," Beth said.

Ramcharger started their second set. During the break, Rick had changed into a red, white and blue Evil Knievel-type outfit. He was having a hard time getting the mic to work with his helmet.

After a while, Kelly walked up to me. She seemed shy around the others, so she leaned up to whisper in my ear that Milo was upset by all the loud music. I told her that maybe she should take Milo into the house—that it might be less noisy in there.

When Kelly walked away, Sara said, "You don't waste any time, do you?" The way she said it she seemed vaguely flirtatious—like she was impressed or something. I guess I could have said the same thing about her.

And that's when I saw Joey. He was wearing full biker regalia and talking to Kelly. Kelly didn't seem too happy about it. She was looking down at her feet and shaking her head. Then she turned and ran around the front of the house.

I decided I better follow her. Joey said, "Hey Keith!" but I kept walking.

I found Kelly sitting on the front steps. She was pressing Milo to her body and talking to herself.

"Kelly?" I said. "Are you okay?"

She shook her head.

"What's wrong?"

"I don't like those people."

"What people?"

"Chad's friends."

"Why not?"

She just shook her head again. She was rocking back and forth now.

I said, "Kelly, I know about the photos."

She stopped rocking and just stared at me with big eyes, which started pooling with tears. Then she stood up and ran away. I got up and was about to chase after her when Dan ran up and grabbed my arm. "Darryl is here."

"What? Where?"

"Nick and that friend of his are fucking with him. Come on."

I followed Dan into the house. We ran into the living room to see Darryl lying prone on the floor. Nick had his knee pressed into the middle of Darryl's back. He was holding a large chrome pistol to Darryl's head.

"Hi Keith," Nick said.

"Nick," I said. "Put the gun away."

"Sure," Nick said. "No problem." But he didn't move.

Tony laughed. His pit bull was growling at Darryl.

"Nick," I said. "I'm not kidding."

Darryl was breathing very quickly. He had his arms out to the side and his face pressed into the rug.

"Hey Darryl," Nick said. "Want to tell us what the fuck you're doing here?"

Darryl didn't say anything.

"Let him go," I said.

Nick looked up at me. Then he looked back at Darryl. "My brother wants me to let you go. The thing is, if I let you go, how do I know you won't come back again and give us a hard time?"

Darryl still didn't say anything. Ramcharger finished a song so it was quiet for a second. But then they started up again.

"Tell you what I'm going to do," Nick said. "If you can say you're sorry to me and my brother, I'll let you go."

Nick removed his knee from Darryl's back and stood up. But he kept his gun pointed at Darryl's head.

Darryl continued to lie face down for a few seconds. Then he sat up. Dirt from the rug was ground into his forehead. He looked very pale and very angry.

"So you gonna apologize or what?" Nick said.

"Nick," I said. "Please shut up."

"Don't tell me to shut up," Nick said. "I'm not your problem." He waved his gun at Darryl's face. "This guy is your problem."

Dan said, "You okay, Darryl?"

Darryl looked at Dan for a second. Then he looked at me. He said, "Fuck you."

"Oh, that's great," Nick said. "Really great." He shook his head like he was disappointed. Then he said, "Look, why don't you get the fuck out of here?" He grabbed Darryl roughly, pulled him up and shoved him toward the door.

Darryl just stood there with his back to us for several seconds. Then he opened the door and walked out.

Nick followed him out the door. "Yeah, yeah. And make it snappy, asshole."

From the front window we all watched as Darryl got in his van, which he had parked up on the sidewalk. After a second, he started the engine and drove off.

Nick walked back inside and closed the door behind him. He smiled. He looked very proud of himself.

I said, "Nice going, Nick."

"Fuck you," Nick said.

"No, fuck you," I said. "This isn't a game. This isn't a movie. Someone could get seriously hurt."

"No fucking shit," Nick said.

"How do you know he won't come back?" I said. "How do you know he's not going to do something really crazy now?"

"I don't," Nick said. "But I think we have an understanding now. I think he realizes that I ain't worth fucking with."

"Hell yeah," Tony said.

He and Nick gave each other a high five.

And that's when the front windows exploded.

We all dove to the floor. Bullets were ricocheting around the room. Chunks of plaster were jumping off the walls. All I could think was that it sounded a lot different that it sounded in movies. It sounded more like weird popping noises, combined with dull thuds and ripping noises within the room. I stayed in a fetal position until it seemed to stop.

When I looked again, the front windows were gone. Nick, Tony, Dan and I were all lying on the floor, covered with bits of plaster and glass.

"Shit," Nick said.

"Damn, man," Tony said. He brushed some plaster off his Charlotte Hornets jacket.

Nick stood up and peeked out over the top of the window frame. "Damn. It's those Asian dudes." Then he said, "Oh shit," and dove to the floor as more bullets sprayed the room.

The weird thing is that, through all of this, Ramcharger kept playing.

"I'm calling the cops," I said.

"No, don't do that," Nick said.

"Too late," I said. I had already dialed 911 on my cell phone. After three rings, someone answered and then immediately put me on hold.

Nick and Tony stood up.

"Man, hang up," Nick said. "They're gone."

I hung up just as the operator came on. That's when I saw Dan. He was in a fetal position and not moving.

"Dan!" I said. "Dan, you okay?"

Dan rolled over. He started feeling his chest and arms. "Yeah," he said. "I think so. Except I think I wet myself."

Just then Chad ran into the room. "What the hell is going on?"

"Nothing, man," Nick said. "Just a bunch of pussy bullshit."

The cops did show up—after just about every neighbor in a four-block radius called 911. By then Ramcharger had stopped playing and the guests had finally started to figure out what had happened. People began leaving in droves.

Strangely enough, Chad didn't seem all that upset. It was as if he thought that this had increased his standing with his friends—like it was the perfect ending for his party. He was all excited, talking to the cops, talking to people as they left. He was showing off a book from his bookcase with a bullet lodged on the inside.

Sara and Beth left without a word to me. Ramcharger left without their equipment. I saw Rick pull away on his motorcycle with the weird feather boa trance-dancing lady clinging to his back. And Dan got out of there with Tammy—I think he was embarrassed about peeing his pants.

Kelly seemed weirdly oblivious to the whole thing. After all the gunfire, she had walked in rather casually, still petting Milo. Actually, she seemed a little too calm—she seemed almost dazed. I wanted to talk to her, but I was having trouble thinking straight. I still had a lot of adrenalin coursing through my system.

By the time the cops finally left, most of the guests had left, too. So it was just me, Nick, Tony, Chad, Melissa and Kelly.

That's when Nick said, "Yo Keith, check your car."

I looked out at my car. The Asian guys had obviously paid special attention to it. It looked like a big piece of Swiss cheese.

"That's great," I said.

Nick said, "Maybe it ain't a hot idea to stick around here tonight."

Chad turned to Melissa. "Could we go to your place for a while?"

Melissa frowned. "I guess."

Twenty

Tony noticed a few bullet holes in his Impala. This put a big damper on his mood and he decided to go home. I was kind of hoping that Nick would go with him, but he didn't. So the rest of us piled into the Explorer, which was safely parked in the garage.

I didn't realize how drunk Chad was until we were on the road. His driving was even worse than usual. I kept thinking we were going to slam into a parked car or go off the road. Chad was happy and oblivious, laughing and shouting drunken observations to Melissa, who seemed strangely subdued in the front passenger seat.

Meanwhile, Nick and I were doing our best to keep Kelly propped up between us. She was holding Milo in her lap and sitting kind of weird—kind of limp. She was like jello. Whenever Chad threw on the brakes she would slump forward and Nick and I would pull her back.

It was past 2 a.m. by the time we got to Melissa's, but no one seemed tired. More like the opposite.

"I'm all jittery," Chad said. He held out his hands, which were trembling. "See, look."

"Tell me about it," Nick said, and shot me a glance.

I felt like it was prom night—like we'd already gotten drunk and been to the dance and had sex and crashed a car and gone to the emergency room and had stitches, but we were still out, waiting for the sun to come up. Why the hell weren't we all in bed?

Then there was Kelly. I was worried about her. She just didn't seem right. She was in her own little world, making cooing noises to Milo. Why hadn't Dan and Tammy taken her home? Was she my responsibility? My brain was too tired. I couldn't think.

And then Nick noticed the boat.

"Hey, is that your boat?" Nick said.

"Yeah," Melissa said.

"Twinkle Toes." Nick laughed. "Hey, let's take it out for a ride!"

"I don't know..." Melissa said.

"Come on, it'll be fun."

"Maybe another time," Melissa said.

"Oh man, come on!" Nick looked at me but I just stared back at him, trying to make my opposition to this idea as obvious as possible.

Then Chad got involved, saying, "Why not? Maybe that's what we all need right now. Some fresh air."

"I think maybe we've had enough excitement for one night," Melissa said.

"Yeah," I said.

"Well, I'll go," Chad said. "If anyone wants to join me they're welcome."

When Chad and Nick headed out to the boat, Kelly got up to follow. It was like she was sleepwalking. I probably should have stayed behind, but I thought I should keep an eye on Kelly. Also, I didn't want to be left alone with Melissa.

Melissa rolled her eyes. "Have fun."

It really was a beautiful night. The sky was clear. You could see all the stars and Lake Union was smooth and glassy.

Kelly went and sat down in the cabin. Nick and I stayed up top as Chad pulled out under the looming freeway and headed toward the lights of the city. The cool night air cleared my head a bit and I was grateful for that. While Nick and Chad were talking about water skiing, I just kind of spaced out.

After a while, Nick went down into the cabin to join Kelly. And so then it was just me and Chad. I was sitting over to the side, watching the patterns that developed in the water, but I noticed that Chad kept looking over at me and smiling. It kind of freaked me out.

Finally, he said, "You don't like me, do you?"

"What?"

"You don't. I can tell."

"What do you mean?" I said. "I like you." But it didn't sound very convincing.

"No you don't," he said, shaking his head. But he was smiling. It was weird. Then he said, "Melissa told me about you two."

I just stared at him.

"Just so you know," he said.

"Okay," I said. I didn't know what to say. Then I said, "So now what?"

"I'm going to have to think about it."

Fair enough. But he seemed to be taking it pretty well—too well, I thought. He kept smiling like he thought it was funny or something. It was creepy.

I was about to go down into the cabin when Nick came back up on deck. "Dude, Kelly is acting kind of weird."

"No shit," I said.

"I gave her some pills to try to mellow her out."

"You gave her some pills?" I said. "What kind of pills?"

"Just some downers," he said. "Don't worry, man."

"Look," I said. "I can't deal with any more shit tonight, okay?"

"Okay, okay. Jeez." Then he said, "Maybe you should talk to her."

"Yeah, alright," I said.

I went below. Kelly was sitting on the little orange bench, crying softly.

I sat down next to her and said, "What's wrong?"

She didn't answer at first, but then she said, "He made me."

"What? Nick?"

She shook her head. "No, not Nick. Chad."

"What are you talking about?"

"The photos," she said, turning to me. "You said you saw them."

Oh shit. I said, "What do you mean he made you?"

She shrugged.

"How did he make you?"

She shook her head.

"Kelly, you can tell me."

But she just kept shaking her head. She didn't want to talk anymore. I tried to put my arm around her but she pulled away.

I sat there for another minute with Kelly but then I felt like I was going to go crazy, so I got up and went back up on deck.

Outside, Nick was showing Chad his gun—the chrome barrel flashing in the moonlight. They were laughing. I couldn't believe it.

I said, "Can I see that for a second?"

Nick just looked at me. Then he shrugged and handed it to me.

It was heavy. I said, "Is it loaded?"

"Yeah it's loaded. Be careful."

I nodded. Then I threw it overboard—threw it casually, like a Frisbee. It spun away and was swallowed by the foamy wake.

"What the fuck?" Nick said.

I shrugged. "Sorry."

Nick looked out at the water. "I can get another one. But you owe me five hundred bucks."

Chad laughed.

I said, "What's so funny?"

"Nothing," Chad said.

"Yeah?" I said. "Kelly just told me about the photos you took of her."

"What are you talking about?"

"You made her pose for your friends. For your porn site."

Chad stopped smiling. But he didn't say anything.

"Yeah, I know all about it. The discs from Joey, the website with the password twinkletoes. Everything."

Chad looked away for a second. Then he shrugged. "So?"

"What do you mean, so?"

"So you've seen it. Big fucking deal." Then he said, "Kelly did it of her own free will. She's an adult."

"Dude," Nick said. He shook his head.

I turned to Nick. "Is that fucked up or what?"

Nick nodded. "That's fucked up."

"Thank you," I said.

Chad just shook his head. "You shouldn't believe everything she tells you."

"No?" I said.

"No," Chad said.

"So what?" I said. "She's lying?"

That question was just kind of hanging there when Kelly came up. She looked awful. Crazy awful. She was shaking and her eyes were all pupil.

"Milo's gone," she said.

We all said, "What?"

"He's gone!" she screamed. She started pulling at her hair. "Help me find him!" She ran back into the cabin.

I looked at Nick. "What exactly did you give her?"

"I told you. Just some downers."

We all looked at each other. Then Nick and I followed her into the cabin.

"Where was he last?" I said.

But Kelly didn't answer. She was throwing vinyl seat cushions and life preservers around the place and making these scary moaning sounds.

Nick and I joined her in the search. But there didn't seem to be anywhere Milo could hide. You can't burrow into plastic.

Soon the cabin floor was a mess of cushions, ropes, buoys, and the scattered contents of a survival kit.

"I'll look up top," I said.

When I got up Chad was smirking and shaking his head. "I told you about her," he said. "She's fucking nuts."

"Fuck you," I said.

"Fuck me?" Chad said. "Fuck you." And with that, he gave me a push. I almost went overboard but managed to catch myself on the railing. And then we were wrestling.

I hadn't been in a fight since third grade, when a big kid named Arnold cut in front of me in line at the handball court. It wasn't even a fight. I just said, "No cuts," and Arnold punched me in the stomach and I doubled over and started crying and that was it.

So basically: I sucked at fighting. And before I knew it, Chad had me pinned.

"I can't believe you fucked Melissa," he said. "She's such a slut."

"Don't call her a slut," I said.

"I'll call her whatever I want," Chad said.

I lunged and managed to push Chad off. "Yeah?" I said, suddenly feeling tough—feeling my Kato super powers swelling. "Come on." I threw Chad back against the wheel.

He said, "Ow, my neck."

I stopped for a second. "You okay?"

"No," he said. But I could tell he was faking.

I laughed. "Oh, is that your motorcycle racing injury? You're so full of shit."

Chad lunged at me again. We were writhing around on the deck when I saw Kelly standing in the doorway, pointing a flare gun at us.

Chad and I froze. "Kelly," I said.

"Stop it," she said. "Stop fighting." She was crying.

"Easy now," I said.

"Where's Milo?" she said. "I want Milo." A very unattractive bit of drool was hanging from her lip. If it had been a movie, that would have been some great fucking method acting.

"I don't know where he is," I said. "But we'll find him."

Kelly lowered the flare gun a bit. She was looking around—looking for Milo.

Then Chad said, "Keith threw him overboard."

"What?" she said.

"What?" I said.

"It's true. He took the little guy and just tossed him. He went ploop!" Chad started giggling maniacally. "Hope Milo knows how to swim."

"Swim?" Kelly said. "Ferrets can't swim." Her eyes were bulging out of her eye sockets.

I turned to Chad. "Are you crazy?"

Chad kept giggling. "I was going to throw him the life preserver, but it's too big for him." Chad couldn't stop himself. He was insane. He was an insane person.

So Kelly shot him.

A flare is kind of like a small rocket. I saw it come out of the gun like a heat-seeking missile. It hit Chad right in the head.

Chad was knocked backwards onto the deck. Almost

immediately, he started writhing, like he was having a seizure. Foamy stuff started coming out of his mouth.

I didn't know what to do. I thought back to the life-saving class I'd had in high school. Mouth to mouth? Don't let him choke on his tongue! But watch your fingers!

Nick appeared in the doorway, holding Milo triumphantly. "I found him!" Then he said, "What the fuck?"

I've never driven a large power boat before but I'm a quick learner. I drove it at fast as I could back to Melissa's houseboat. The bow lifted way up in the air and a white wake spooled out behind us.

Kelly had fainted. Nick was going back and forth between her and Chad.

"This is bad," he said.

"No shit," I said.

I think Melissa knew something was up. She was waiting out on the dock as we approached.

I tried to slow down—I slammed it into reverse, causing water to churn violently behind us—but we ended up hitting the deck hard, sideways. Nick was thrown off the boat and onto the dock. He was up almost immediately, hopping on one foot. "Ow, ow!"

"What happened?" Melissa said.

"Kelly shot Chad with a flare gun," I said.

"What?!"

"I think he had a seizure."

"Oh my god," she said. "His neck."

Chad looked bad. The flare had burned his forehead. It looked like he was missing an eyebrow. Plus, he wasn't moving.

Of course we've all heard that you're not supposed to move someone in Chad's condition. Just like we've all heard that you shouldn't run out of buildings when there's an earthquake, that you shouldn't panic in a fire, that you shouldn't go swimming right after a big meal. But Chad looked dead. We couldn't wait. We had to do something.

Nick, Melissa and I half-carried, half-dragged Chad to the Explorer and laid him out in the back. Then Melissa and I jumped in. Nick limped back to the boat to check on Kelly and Milo.

I was driving. I didn't know where we were going, but Melissa was in back yelling at me to hurry.

At first I was slowing down for stop lights but there was almost no one on the road and Melissa just kept yelling at me to go faster. So I started blowing lights. It was kind of cool in a way. I kept my foot down, kept it floored, and right then and there I decided that for my next job I was going to be a paramedic. I'd be good at it. It would be perfect—I wouldn't have to work in a cubicle but I'd still make decent money and I could get my own apartment. And I'd be doing something real for once in my life.

By the time I saw the Rainier truck start to turn in our direction it was too late. I hit it head on.

I think I blacked out. When I woke up, I heard Melissa sobbing behind me. I was covered with white shit—this weird white powder shit. I couldn't figure out what it was but then I realized that it was from the airbag.

I guess the truck driver was okay because he did one of those superman things and ripped my door off its hinges.

"Are you alright?" he said. He looked like a lumberjack.

"I don't know," I said.

Melissa was still sobbing behind me. I couldn't turn around to look.

"Jesus Christ," the guy said. "Don't move." He ran around to the back of the Explorer.

I felt very light. I went to undo my seatbelt. I kept feeling around for the buckle. It took me a while to realize that it wasn't on—I hadn't put it on.

The next thing I knew I was walking. Just walking. Walking down the sidewalk. I remembered a Christmas special from when I was a kid. It involved a monster. A Christmas monster? Anyway, at the end of the movie, the monster sang a little song. It went: "Just put one foot in front of the other, and soon you'll be walking out the door-or-or..." It was a nice tune. A tune you could hum or sing along to.

I could hear sirens.

I started shaking my head, no, no, no. No police. Police meant I was going to need my I.D. "License and registration, please." But they all knew me. I was Kato. Kato Kaelin. Or was I? No. I was the other guy. Remember? The guy who was driving the Explorer. No, the Bronco. The white Bronco. Right. What was his name? The football player. The black football player. O.J.'s friend. Al something. Al

Cowlings. Yeah, I was Al Cowlings. Yeah, that's the ticket. Al Cowlings. Al? A cow?

No. I shook my head, no, no. I'm a white guy. I'm Kato. Kato Kaelin.

A police car pulled up next to me.

"Hey you," the voice said. "Stop."

I stopped. I looked around. Where the hell was I? I saw trees and bushes and houses.

Someone was shining a flashlight in my eyes.

"I think you need to sit down."

There were hands on me. A laying on of hands.

I was sitting on the curb with a blanket over me. The blanket was warm but I couldn't feel it. It itched slightly. Was it wool? Wool itches.

A nice-looking woman cop was peering into my face. She had rosy cheeks.

"Hi," she said. "How are you?"

"Okay," I said. "Tired."

"Have you been drinking?"

"Yes." I shook my head. "No."

"Can you tell me your name?"

"My name?" I said.

"Yes, your name." She was smiling. She seemed so nice. Pretty and nice.

"Um," I said.

"You can't remember your name?" she said. And then it was like she was getting farther and farther away from me. But she was so nice. I wanted to be nice, too.

"Let's try one more time," she said. "What is your name?"

"It's Kato," I said. "Kato Kaelin."

Twenty-One

I stopped over in Salt Lake City on my way to Colorado. The day before I'd gone to the junkyard with Dan and Carl. We found a new door for the Celica to replace the one that had been filled with bullet holes. We found a seat, too. The door was green and the seat was maroon, but what the hell, they worked.

I'd been released from the hospital after a day. They said I'd only had a slight concussion and some bruised ribs. It hurt when I breathed.

Melissa got off with a sprained wrist and some minor bruising. Chad had some severe burns from the flare gun but otherwise he seemed okay. A CAT scan and MRI had been done and everything checked out. However, they were going to keep him under observation for a week or so as a precaution.

A newspaper article came out about the various incidents of that night, and the reporter even tried to link the shooting at the house to the car accident. Chad came off as a shady, mysterious figure—there was no mention of the porn site, but as it turned out, he was still being sued over some of his father's old business dealings. I was listed as the driver of the vehicle. There were no Kato jokes.

After getting out of the hospital, I spent a few miserably boring days at my parents' house alone (by the time I called them from the hospital, they had already left for Tibet). While I was there, Nick called to tell me that it was over between me and Kelly—that Kelly never wanted to see me again. When I asked him about his relationship with Kelly, he was evasive. He did say that he was taking Milo down to school with him, that he was "starting to like the little dude."

I talked to Sara a few times. She and Beth were having problems and Beth was moving out. Again I heard the sound of possibility in her voice, the vague longing for something we had once had. But I had already decided to leave—in my mind I was already gone.

So I called my dad in Colorado. It was good to talk to him after years of zero communication. As it turned out, he had given up the kayak instructor thing and was working as a contractor. Business was booming, he said, and if I wanted, he could get me some work. And so I agreed, picturing myself with a sunburn and a leather tool belt, standing in the wood frames of new houses high above green valleys and shimmering mountain lakes.

I slept late, and the motel parking lot was empty by the time I walked out to my car. Hearing the semis rumbling past, I suddenly felt impatient to be on my way. I got coffee and a candy bar from the hotel vending machines, and minutes later, I was merging onto I-80, urging the old Celica east.